people with no charisma

people with no charisma

Jente Posthuma

Translated by Sarah Timmer Harvey

Melbourne | London | Minneapolis

Scribe Publications
18–20 Edward St, Brunswick, Victoria 3056, Australia
2 John St, Clerkenwell, London, WC1N 2ES, United Kingdom
3754 Pleasant Ave, Suite 223w, Minneapolis, Minnesota 55409, USA

Published by Scribe 2025
Published by arrangement with Van Grunsven Creative Management, originally published by Atlas Contact, Amsterdam

Copyright © Jente Posthuma 2016
Translation copyright © Sarah Timmer Harvey 2025

All rights reserved. Without limiting the rights under copyright reserved above, no part of this publication may be reproduced, stored in or introduced into a retrieval system, or transmitted, in any form or by any means (electronic, mechanical, photocopying, recording or otherwise) without the prior written permission of the publishers of this book.

The moral rights of the author and translator have been asserted.

Typeset in Adobe Garamond by the publishers.

Printed and bound in the UK by CPI Group (UK) Ltd, Croydon CR0 4YY

Scribe is committed to the sustainable use of natural resources and the use of paper products made responsibly from those resources.

978 1 761381 34 8 (Australian edition)
978 1 917189 03 3 (UK edition)
978 1 964992 21 1 (US edition)
978 1 761386 27 5 (ebook)

Catalogue records for this book are available from the National Library of Australia and the British Library.

This project has been assisted by the Australian Government through Creative Australia, its arts funding and advisory body.

scribepublications.com.au
scribepublications.co.uk
scribepublications.com

The Pyromaniac and His Labrador

My father dug an enormous spoonful of yoghurt and muesli out of a bowl, opened his mouth wide and stuck the spoon inside. The muesli cracked between his teeth. Occasionally, his mouth would open and close, producing smacking sounds. The swallowing of each mouthful was accompanied by a distinctly audible tightening of the muscles in his throat, followed by a dull click and a sigh.

The sun was shining. It wasn't terribly warm, but it was still early. The afternoon was supposed to be considerably warmer. I was already wearing my bikini underneath my dress and pretending to fiddle with my hair, but I was actually rubbing my ears. After a while, I dropped the pretence and continued rubbing. In the meantime, I was watching my father. He looked back at me briefly and continued eating. His scoops of muesli were so big that heaps of it would fall off the spoon before it even reached his mouth. Sometimes he'd notice it happening and try to catch the crumbs with his tongue.

I went out to the swimming pool in the backyard and sat on the edge of it, dangling my legs in the cold water. Water was streaming into the pool from the elevated fibreglass wall. If I closed my eyes, it was almost like sitting beside a babbling brook in the forest. Then the neighbour stuck her head over the fence.

'Lovely, isn't it?' she called. She was an educator.

I stood up and went back inside. My father was still sitting there, but now he had a toothpick in his mouth.

'You may walk the dog,' he said almost inaudibly, with a grimace.

'Must,' I said, 'not may.'

Outside, the boy who lived next door was smashing a TV with a metal shovel. He liked to dismantle old televisions, then try to rebuild them. If they failed to work, he'd smash them to pieces. That boy was very strong. 'He has lots of energy,' his mother would say. Occasionally, he and I would get into a scuffle in the front yard. I'd kick his shins until he pushed me over. Even though he was only eleven, two years younger than me, he could do that quite easily.

The dog ran up to him and thrust its nose into his crotch from behind.

'Stop that!' I yelled at the dog, then waved at the boy,

who sprang into the air with his hands on his bum.

Our street was a cul-de-sac attached to a long boulevard. It was basically a little lane where four identical bungalows had been built. Behind the bungalows was a public field. My dog liked to poop there, and while he was doing his business, I'd practise gymnastics on the monkey bars. A pyromaniac lived quite close by, in one of the townhouses along the boulevard. One night, when his parents weren't home, he lit his house on fire. The whole neighbourhood came out to see the fire and it made the evening news.

'Tobias was the first to notice the fire,' the pyromaniac told the reporter. Tobias was his black Labrador. The dog had started barking when smoke began to appear under the kitchen pantry door. 'Thankfully, otherwise I wouldn't be here anymore.'

'It wouldn't surprise me if he was the one who started it,' my father said immediately afterwards. And he was right, which I thought was amazing. It was then that I understood why my father was the head of a psychiatric institution. He saw right through people. My father couldn't read people's minds in the way that some of his more gullible patients seemed to believe, but he was a sharp observer. For instance, I could see him easily figuring out the secrets behind a magician's tricks, simply by refusing to look at the hand that was holding out something for him to see and keeping an eye on the other hand instead. My father never paid much attention to what was happening right under his nose.

The dog had finished pooping but was lingering on

the field. I imagined the pyromaniac walking past with his Labrador. He sometimes used to ring our doorbell and ask if I wanted to come and smoke with him. We'd tie the dogs to the monkey bars and then smoke a cigarette together in the bushes at the edge of the field. We'd always smoke Roxy Dual extra lights, his mother's brand.

He often called her 'the cunt', which I found funny. He called me 'silly goose'. I'd never seen him light anything except cigarettes, apart from the time he'd held a Zippo beside his bum and farted. The blowtorch this created lit a few leaves on fire, but we'd managed to put it out within seconds. Another time, he'd suddenly lowered his face to mine and tried to kiss me. In a panic, I'd turned my ear to his mouth.

'What did you say?' I asked. It tingled when his cheek brushed mine. He swallowed close to my ear, and I could hear his saliva passing through his oesophagus very clearly. Long after this happened, after the fire, I heard that he used to douse live mice with petrol and light them on fire. Now he was in an institution. Not the one my father ran, a different one, for teenagers with behavioural issues.

I decided to take a longer walk, through the park and the shopping centre, then back again. The only thing open at the shopping centre was the fast-food place. It was the same place we ordered from every Sunday. Hot chips for me and breaded sausages with curry sauce for my father. He adored them. My mother didn't, but my mother was dead.

She was incredibly thin, my mother. There were times when dry bread was all she would eat and days when she consumed only little cups of pudding. Her legs were perpetually tanned, even in the winter. If there was ever a hint of sun, you'd find her tanning her slim legs in the garden. When the sun was particularly fierce, beads of sweat would run down the length of her calves. On hot days, I'd usually lie in the shade, with a towel covering my entire body to keep away the insects.

'Come out from underneath that towel,' my mother would often say, 'come and lie next to me in the sun. You're so pale.' I'd go and lie next to her, beads of sweat gathering on my calves, and that's where I'd stay, even if it made me feel like I was suffocating. If I really couldn't stand it anymore, I'd walk to the kitchen with dark spots dancing before my eyes to get an ice cream. I'd always eat it in the garage where my mother wouldn't see me. She could look at people who walked around eating ice creams, crisps and hot chips with such disdain. When she got sick, her body swelled up and the medicine turned her skin light yellow.

'You're still a very beautiful woman,' I declared one day after finding her collapsed on the banquette in front of the large mirror in the hall. She looked even puffier than usual because she'd been crying. I was the one she asked to choose an outfit for her to be buried in because she said I had outstanding taste, just like her. I chose a blue Italian dress, with a subtle floral pattern. When I tried to put it on her after she died, I had to cut open the sleeves at the back of the dress to make it fit.

For a moment, I considered picking up the chips and breaded sausages right away, but we wouldn't eat for another few hours. And you can't reheat hot chips. My father didn't know these kinds of things. He put everything in the microwave. Ever since my mother had died, he'd taken to buying ready-made pancakes at the supermarket. He warmed them up one by one in the microwave and would eat each pancake as soon as it was ready, standing at the kitchen counter.

When I got home my father was watching the Grand Prix in Monaco live on TV. I could hear the F1 cars screeching even before I entered the house. I brought the dog inside, then walked straight through to the garden. Once outside, I stepped out of my dress and let myself sink into the pool. The water had already warmed up. I dove down, then resurfaced and dove again, trying to stay underwater as long as possible. The water pump was the only thing I could hear. It made a bubbling sound, which was different from the sound my mother made just before she died. That had been more of a gurgle.

People with No Charisma

I'd just turned eight and was allowed to go to the theatre to see Goethe's *Faust*. My mother was appearing in it. She was playing one of the whores that Mephisto, the devil, gave to Professor Faust in exchange for his soul.

'Don't be shocked,' she said, because I would be seeing her bare breasts and someone other than my father would be touching them. My father stayed at home to watch the dog. We'd only just gotten the dog, and we weren't able to leave him alone because he'd get nervous and poop on the rug.

But it wouldn't shock me at all because I'd seen my mother naked a million times. At home, and during our camping trips in the south of France. Everyone there walked around naked, though I preferred to wear my disco suit: a pair of pink, shiny hotpants and a pink camisole with the word DISCO written across it in purple letters.

I was dressed in my most beautiful dress for the performance. It was red and almost floor-length.

'You look faaaabulous,' said my mother, like only a real actress could, but she seemed quite distracted.

We stood beside each other in front of the mirror. Just like my mother, I turned and peered over my shoulder to see how I looked from behind. I was quite pleased. My mother smoothed her dress and asked if I thought it suited her. Her backside also got my approval.

'Really?' she asked. Now I had her attention. I nodded, smiling widely at her in the mirror.

'You're a beautiful whore,' said my father. He grabbed my mother's hips, but she pushed him away from her.

'The taxi's here!' she cried. My mother had ordered a taxi just for me.

On the way to the theatre, she told me about all the people I would meet and reminded me to shake hands with the two famous actors who were playing the lead roles. I was supposed to look them in the eye and say, 'Lovely to meet you,' and nothing else, so I wouldn't break their focus. I could speak freely with all the other actors, she said. As long as I didn't talk to them about my school assignments, because artists don't find that kind of thing very interesting. Grades mean nothing to me, my mother always said. What's important is how you express yourself to the world. 'Show yourself!' she would shout, spreading her arms wide. She also talked a lot about charisma, and particularly about people who didn't have any. People with no charisma were terrible people, they were even worse than ugly people. Every day, my mother would pick me up from school and when I'd see her through the classroom window, standing by the gate in her knee-high boots and second-hand fur coat, I would put all my energy into radiating charisma. I'd flex my muscles and tense my jaw until my head began to buzz. Then I would try to walk outside as expressively as possible.

On the way back from my first school trip the previous year, when the bus was just about to turn into the school parking lot, all the other kids giggled and dove under their seats. 'Come on, you should hide too!' they'd cried, but I was the only one who stayed in my seat. I wanted my mother to see me coming from a distance, to have my charisma arrive before the bus did.

There was a bowl filled with fun-sized Mars bars in the dressing room at the theatre. I was allowed to take as many as I wanted.

'Don't hold back, sweetie,' everyone kept saying. There was cola too, and they urged me to keep drinking it, even though I was still quite full from dinner. When my mother called for me, I quickly finished the rest of my cola. It was time to shake hands with the lead actors. They laughed loudly when I said, 'Lovely to meet you.' You could say they roared with laughter.

'Well,' I said, 'my mother told me to say that.' Then my mother started roaring too.

'We're laughing *with* youuuuuu,' she cried as I walked away with my arms crossed and my eyes on the floor.

I left the dressing room and, without looking up, walked until I reached a passageway between two dark curtains. At the end of the passage, a fire marshal was sitting on a folding chair behind a folding table. He was drinking coffee out of a plastic cup.

'Young lady,' he said in a stern voice, 'what are you doing here?'

He startled me.

'I've come to see my mother,' I said and ran away from him up the passageway.

'Wait, wait!' he called after me. 'Where's your mother then?'

I wasn't sure anymore. Rounding a corner, I arrived in a cluttered room. There were stacks of wooden chairs beside several black crates and on top of the crates were three trolls. They weren't real trolls, but I still didn't dare to walk past them, and I didn't want to go back to the fire marshal either, so I stayed where I was. The trolls stared at me, grinning through the darkness, and I began to cry. I stood there until, out of nowhere, I heard my mother calling me from behind the only door in the room. She barged through the door wearing a bright blue dressing gown, her lips painted deep red and her eyes rimmed in black.

'There you are,' she said. 'Why are you hiding again? Hurry up, we're about to start!'

I was allowed to watch the play from the front row. The

soft, red plush chair felt unbelievably luxurious. I decided not to sit on the cushion that my mother had given me. Instead, I pulled it into my lap and wrapped my arms around it as if it was a teddy bear.

The houselights dimmed, the curtains opened, and the performance began. One of the two famous actors whose hands I had shaken was painted entirely black and had pointy ears. He was Mephisto. Another, less famous actor was playing God in a glittery outfit that reminded me a little of my disco suit, except his pants were long instead of short and white instead of pink. Mephisto growled and cackled. Then Professor Faust appeared. He was played by the other actor who had roared with laughter. Onstage, he mostly screamed. Every now and then, a woman would join the others, and she screeched so loudly I felt embarrassed and had to cover my ears and bury my head in the cushion. Faust looked admiringly at the screeching woman. The devil also found her pretty. I didn't understand that because my mother was much prettier. But she would only appear later in the play. I didn't know exactly when. Her name was printed in the programme in the list of names under the word 'whores'. My mother was incredibly pleased with this role, her first since she'd had me. Before that, she'd been in a few plays and TV shows and would occasionally get recognised on the street, but that didn't happen anymore.

'I have to get this right,' she kept saying. 'If I don't make an impression now, then it will never happen, and I'll want to die.' My mother often said that she wanted to die. Right before the premiere, she'd walked through the house like a ghost, and I'd never seen her so lacking in charisma.

To cheer her up, I kept telling her that she was the most beautiful person in the world. My father tried to calm her by saying it wasn't so bad, that she would appear onstage very briefly and only had a few lines, but this made her angry. Once, I asked her why she was so scared. She laughed and said, 'I'm never scared.'

In the meantime, I was getting nervous. When would the whores appear? I was also trying to ignore the fact that I really needed to pee. I thought about sneaking through the auditorium to the toilets in the foyer, but the space behind me was too dark to make out the exit. And anyway, I couldn't leave. My mother would be terribly disappointed if I missed her performance. She had brought me with her for a reason and the taxi had been expensive. I jiggled my legs.

'Think about our holiday,' my father would say whenever I wasn't feeling well and that's exactly what I did. I thought about ladybirds and the way my disco suit shimmered in the bright sun, the big glass jar full of caramels at the campsite store, and the long line of naked holidaymakers standing at the check-out. The cashier and I were often the only ones wearing any clothes.

But thinking about all that now wasn't helping, I really had to go. I tensed my muscles until my whole body was shaking. Onstage, a choir of angels had started singing. Their voices sounded high, light and enchanting. And that's when I wet myself. It felt strange, almost like a dream. At first my seat felt warm, but it quickly turned cold and clammy. I thought that if I stayed very still it was possible no one would notice, so I stared straight in front of me and hugged the cushion even tighter.

Imagine if my mother came onstage right now, I thought, and saw me sitting in a pool of my own piss. What if it shocked her? I could ruin everything and then she would want to die.

'Please God,' I whispered, 'make me invisible.' Maybe he could hide me in one of those black crates and put a troll on top of it. As the screaming onstage grew louder, I pressed my face deeper and deeper into the cushion. Everything was muffled and even the sharp scent of urine seemed to dissipate.

Startled by a strange whinnying, I looked up to see my mother disappearing backstage. Mephisto growled and groped the air behind her. God watched from a distance in his white disco suit. Why doesn't he do anything, I thought, then walked carefully through the darkness to the exit.

'Did you enjoy it?' asked my mother in the foyer after it was over. She took a long sip of her wine and looked restlessly around the room. My red dress had dried, but it still smelt weird, and my legs felt very sticky. I awkwardly shifted, putting some distance between us as I considered my answer.

'Yes,' I said eventually.

In the meantime, my mother had turned her back to me and was looking at the door through which the lead actors were now entering the foyer. She waved.

'Over here, guys!' she called. They waved back and then walked over to the bar, where they greeted the actress who had been screeching so loudly onstage. The actress was very cheerful. While she was talking, she kept touching the arm of the actor playing Mephisto, who had taken the seat next to hers.

'That woman drinks too much,' said my mother, 'then does strange things.' I imagined the actress pissing all over her beautiful suit and the barstool and was relieved when my mother suggested we go home.

Christmas Story

On Christmas Eve, my mother could always be found in the garage, flapping her hands in front of her face. This was her way of keeping her tears at bay. Every year she bought a guinea fowl and stuffed it with a mixture of minced veal, homemade truffle, and chantarelle mushrooms she had bought at a farmers' market in a village nearby. She had to bike all the way there because my father always had the car during the day. And every year she'd take the bird out of the oven and say it was a disaster. This made me angry, because her roast guinea fowl was delicious. Sometimes, just to see how she would react, I would tell her that the guinea fowl was indeed a disaster but it wasn't so bad.

The first time I'd got that angry at her, I grabbed half a loaf of bread, a packet of sliced ham, a hunk of cheese, put it all in my bindle and went out into the world. I was around nine years old. I'd made my bindle out of an old dress, an elastic band and a stick, just like the children in my favourite book had done. In the book, four children, two brothers and two sisters, travelled through New Jersey after their mother left them in a parking lot. They tried to spend the small amount of money they had as sensibly as possible. The author regularly gave an overview of the things they bought, which was usually a large jar of peanut butter, some bread and four apples. I liked knowing how much bread they had left at the end of the day and how long it would take them to finish the jar of peanut butter. When they were cold, they'd buy frankfurters and tinned ravioli, because it was cheap and easy to heat over a fire. If they happened to make a disastrous meal, they were able to tell each other without it ruining the mood. In any case, they never said a meal was bad just to fish for compliments.

That Christmas Eve, when I went outside with my bindle, the world was blanketed with snow. Faint light from a lamppost cast the jungle gym and field of poop behind our house in a romantic light. I'd worked out that I should be able to make the bread, ham and cheese last three days if I skipped lunch. And I could make water by letting snow melt in my hands. Inside the neighbour's bungalow, their son was standing on a stool at the kitchen counter while his mother prepared Christmas dinner. He was pounding his fists into a lump of dough. I went and stood under the lantern pole and waited for him to see me, but he didn't look my way. I have to get going, I thought. Then my father came outside.

'Shall we take a little walk?' he asked. After dinner, we played three rounds of Ludo and I was allowed to stay up extra late.

My mother hated it when I called her a liar. She said it felt like the ground falling away beneath her feet. Which is why I decided to believe all her lies. The only time that didn't work was during Christmas, especially if we had guests.

For days in advance she'd be stressed and would lash out at my father if she caught him picking his nose or wearing socks that were too short. She'd sigh repeatedly and say there was still so much left to do and that she wasn't looking forward to having guests, even though it had been her idea to invite them in the first place. And she was already having trouble sleeping. The dark circles under her eyes were growing more difficult to camouflage by the day. I often found her in front of the mirror, whining because she thought she was too fat. If I was to believe my mother, everything about her was a total disaster.

She really wanted me to be special, a child prodigy like Mozart, or even Jesus. She did her absolute best to get everyone to believe that I was special. But if you are disastrous yourself, then your child is also likely to be born a disaster. That's just the way it is.

My father wasn't that much of a success either. My mother said that she could have got a much better husband, including a Native American man from Wisconsin who owned hotels on several continents. But she chose my father after all, a lanky Dutch medical student who wore thick glasses. She met him in a café she frequented when she was young. He was working at the bar to earn some extra money. He wasn't a handsome barman. He wasn't even particularly charming. She couldn't emphasise that enough. He was an unremarkable barman who cleaned the bar diligently and always filled up her glass at exactly the right moment, while more successful men vied for her attention. The Native American man invited her to come live with him in New York. He was planning to take over the Chelsea Hotel. And he knew Bob Dylan, had even spoken with him more than once.

'Were you too scared to go?' I asked my mother years later.

'Of course not,' she said.

My father played a lot of Bob Dylan at the café. The night that the Native American man left for good, my father sang along softly to the music. He knew all the lyrics by heart, and to impress my mother, he sang each line just before Dylan did, as if he were the one prompting the singer. It worked. That was the evening my mother finally looked up and noticed him. Two years later she moved with him into a brick bungalow in an outer suburb, next to a poop field where there was a jungle gym for her child, because I was already on the way.

○

Whenever we had guests at Christmas, my mother's lies spiralled out of control. She laughed at everything, even when it was clear she wasn't feeling very good, especially when the guinea fowl had been a disaster.

'I swear it's usually much tastier, I swear,' she always said.

'But isn't it always a disaster?' I once asked, surprised.

She'd laughed again and pinched me under the table so hard that tears sprang into my eyes.

After my mother had accepted everyone's compliments on the meal, she'd usually turn the conversation to me and the last exceptionally beautiful story I'd written. She really loved stories.

'Come on, read it for us.' Generally, she would say this at least once a month, or whenever we had guests. And if I didn't want to do it, she'd pressure me. 'Please,' she'd keep saying. 'Do it for me.' Our guests, who usually leaned back indulgently when she first mentioned it, would begin to shift uneasily in their seats and, to save face for my mother, I'd eventually stand up and do it. With one fist clenched behind my back I'd read a story about the death of my goldfish or an orphan who had only four euro fifty to their name or something about the Nazis and the Holocaust. But at Christmas dinner, as we sat there with our antique silver knife rests and serviette rings, between the coloured lights and paper angels, it all became too much for me. 'Do it yourself!' I'd scream at her. 'Write your own stupid story!' After that, my mother would go into the garage and flap her hands in front of her face.

A few years later, I discovered that my mother wasn't a disaster at all. Looking at old photos, I also realised that she wasn't fat. And in a wardrobe, beneath her underpants, I discovered a lined notebook full of stories she'd written. Her writing was beautiful. 'Liar!' I yelled, but she couldn't hear me. She was lying downstairs in the living room in a hospital bed. My father had asked me to fetch some underpants because it was time to change her.

In one of her stories, my mother described how she would deliberately show her mother, my grandmother, the obituaries of young people who had died, just so she could watch her weep. My grandmother cried easily, even when it came to the obituaries of Satan's children, who didn't believe in the Truth. My mother and her parents were believers. The three of them would go door-to-door spreading the word of Jehovah. 'Get lost,' people would say. My mother thought this was normal at the time. Later, she would have heated discussions about religion with her parents at the dinner table. She began to find their beliefs ludicrous and hypocritical. Once, in a fit of rage, she threw a herring at the wallpaper. It left a large greasy stain.

Only Jehovah's Witnesses who did their absolute best would live forever in the heavenly paradise. 'It's obviously nonsense,' my mother once said, 'and still, I wouldn't be surprised if it turned out there's a heavenly paradise after all.' When she got pregnant accidentally, she could no longer enter paradise. She became a child of Satan who was guilty of the sin of fornication. And while her parents weren't allowed to have any contact with her, they initially continued to let her visit them. If a brother or sister from the church happened to ring the doorbell, my mother would take me and sneak out the back door. I don't remember that anymore. All I can recall is that my grandfather could make coins magically disappear and that he often asked me to 'pull his finger'. When I was about five, my grandparents became more religious and cut off all contact with us. A few days before my mother died, they suddenly appeared at our door.

'It could still happen,' my grandmother sobbed. If my mother would just say, 'I'm sorry, Jehovah,' then she could still enter the heavenly paradise. My mother turned her head away. My father moistened her lips with a plant mister.

'She can't apologise,' I said, 'because she would be lying.' I saw my mother moving her arms restlessly and pulled the blanket over her shoulders. She must be cold, I thought, but her hands quickly reappeared above the blanket. They were searching for something. It was only when I covered her hands with mine that they stopped.

I Knew No One

My graduation ceremony wasn't a big deal: my father wore new shoes, people drank coffee out of plastic cups, and the vice principal read out the names of the graduating students into a microphone. When my name was called, I shook hands with the principal and vice principal and accepted my diploma. My father took a photo. Embarrassed, I assumed an exaggerated pose.

After the ceremony, my French teacher congratulated me. He asked about my plans for the future while continuously stirring his coffee with a wooden stirrer. During my first year of high school, a few girls in my class had complained to the vice principal because they felt that he bent over them too closely when correcting their work. 'He's just a little bit clumsy,' I'd wanted to say to those girls at the time.

I told him I was going to Paris to write a book. I thought that was sure to please him. When he stopped stirring to tell me all about his favourite French writers, I forgot to pay attention, but did notice that he sounded elated.

I knew a real writer. He wore lambswool sweaters and used words like 'cerebral' and 'presumably'. Every Wednesday afternoon, he'd come to the Cannabis Café where I worked.

'Can I have a pre-rolled Jamaica Gold?' he'd ask the house dealer.

'Well, all right then,' the house dealer would say.

'You always look right at me when I walk in,' the writer said when we were lying in bed together for the first time. 'It's the best part of my Wednesday.'

Eventually, the best part of his Wednesday shifted to the evenings, when we'd have sex on his sofa or in his bed. We'd talk and drink wine until I could barely keep my eyes open.

He knew a lot about philosophy. Sometimes I took notes.

'The soul is what is "mine",' I read afterward in my notebook. It was written crookedly across the page in my drunken handwriting. 'If you are talking about "my life", "my love", or "my depression", then that is the soul talking. Desire is related to "I". It is the rational part. You can say "I want to be happy", and still not be happy. The soul decides. Your desire determines only what will open your soul and what you choose to shut out.'

I can only remember fragments of those Wednesday nights. The way he looked at me when I said something funny, and how he kissed and did his best not to look too proud of himself after showing me his party trick. He could produce the sound of two hands clapping simply by shaking one of his hands. His plumber had taught him how to do it.

The writer lived on the top floor of the tallest apartment building in the city, just behind the shopping centre. He never had to close his curtains. Between the bookshelves in his living room, there was a large wooden cupboard full of shelves and little drawers. Once, he pulled a butt plug out of one of the drawers. 'Don't worry, I cleaned it,' he said. Another time, he stuck his hand into a different drawer and grabbed a little envelope full of coke. He told me he loved me that night. I got goosebumps and my eyes started burning, because I knew that he meant it.

His girlfriend and their daughter lived in a commune in another part of the city. He went to visit them every weekend. The writer said that he didn't want to have to choose between her and me. He quoted ancient and contemporary philosophers when talking about the meaning of individual freedom, personal independence and the art of living. You should never be beholden to a lover, family member or employer, he said.

I remembered everything he told me about his girlfriend, and considered all those little pieces of information clues that I used to reconstruct a picture of the life they shared.

Their car was a light green Simca. She always drove, and he'd sit beside her. Her family were farmers and she was the youngest of nine. The two oldest kids had a different father. She liked beef jerky and white wine. If they ever had to stand in a long queue, she'd walk away, even if it was the line for the red carpet at the National Literary Gala. She had big boobs and a good sense of humour.

There was a portrait of his girlfriend and their child hanging above the writer's desk. His girlfriend had tiny, bright blue eyes that were so close together she looked cross-eyed. Their daughter had inherited the same eyes.

Sometimes, I'd ride my bike past the girlfriend's house after school, hoping to catch a glimpse of her. I never saw her, but one day I did spot their Simca. The backseat was littered with sweet wrappers and on the front passenger seat was the book review section from the previous day's newspaper, with something scribbled on it in his handwriting. And there it is, I thought. So they do see each other during the week. Later, he claimed that they'd just gone to IKEA together to buy a new bed for their kid.

'Sorry that I have a child,' he said.

When I passed my final exams, I decided that I too wanted to be free and independent.

'I'm going to Paris,' I said, 'to write a book.'

There was a part of me that hoped he would convince me not to go. He was quiet for a moment. On the roof of the shopping centre, two pigeons were taking turns picking at an empty chocolate wrapper.

'Very well,' was the response. 'Go and write a book in Paris.'

My new home was the former servants' quarters on the top floor of a chic apartment complex in the seventh arrondissement. My landlady was an old woman who lived on the second floor. The room was small and musty, but it had a relatively large roof deck with a view of the courtyard. I could also see the Eiffel Tower from the roof deck, which was only one hundred metres away and cast a shadow over the entire block in the afternoons.

It was August and quite warm. Every day, I walked aimlessly through the city until my legs were numb and my back was soaked in sweat. My father called often. In the beginning, we mostly talked about practicalities: whether I'd already hung up the towel hooks he'd given me. 'If you're not able to do it yourself, do you know anyone who could do it for you?' he asked. I knew no one, I said. If I tried to tell him anything, he'd talk over me and every time it fell silent, we'd both say: 'Okay, good.'

My father preferred not to get too involved in my upbringing while my mother was still alive. It was only when I was facing serious problems that he'd talk things over with me. He'd speak to me the same way he spoke to his patients at the psychiatric institution: calmly and full of understanding. For instance, when I stopped eating a few years ago, and spent every evening scraping as much food as I could from my plate onto a piece of aluminium foil I kept on my lap. Then I would throw the ball of foil-covered food in the garbage bin behind the house. I kept this up for a few weeks until my mother asked what I was doing. She sounded so dismayed that I burst into tears and ran to my room. A little later, my father came to find me, and we talked about my mother's slowly growing tumours and her bald head. It still startled me to come across her lying on the couch in the late afternoon twilight. She reminded me of Nosferatu from the old black-and-white film I'd once watched at school, but without the pointy ears.

'Sometimes I wish she would die,' I said, 'just so I could take a break from it all.'

I studied my father's face. He nodded. And I started to cry again. My father gave me a packet of tissues he'd evidently brought with him.

'I usually cry at night,' he said. We talked a little longer about the food and the aluminium foil, and he advised me to set myself several small goals each day, like getting out of bed early, making my bed, and completing my homework before a certain time. Every time I achieved one of these goals, I would feel like I was in control of my life again.

In the months following my mother's death, my father and I would only exchange essential information. I lived in the guest quarters, with my own bathroom and toilet. We greeted each other in the mornings in the kitchen. And he'd leave a plate of food for me on the counter every evening. He usually sat in the living room, watching television while playing solitaire on his computer, which he had brought in from his study for that specific purpose.

Before I left for Paris, my father arranged everything for me: a room with a telephone, pocket money, phrase books, and towel hooks with special glue on the back so they wouldn't fall off the wall if I hung heavy towels on them. He also tried to insist on driving me to Paris in his car, but I refused his offer. I wanted to be independent. All he had to do was pay for my train ticket.

'It's your Papaaaa,' he'd say when he was feeling upbeat. My father usually called me around ten in the evening, once he'd had a cognac or two. After a few phone calls, he loosened up a bit and dared to broach more personal subjects. Eventually, he began to skip small talk altogether and just started telling me things without asking if it was convenient. He admitted that he sometimes found it difficult without my mother, especially in the evenings when he came home and there was no one to complain to about his patients. There was one patient who would invent new ways of committing suicide every week. His latest project was a customised machine that would only react to the sound of his voice. When he said a particular code word, one of the machine's arms would begin to move. The arm would push a lever that would set a model train in motion, which would then run over the rails until it broke a string that was attached to a bucket hanging over his bed, and the bucket would tip and spill its contents all over him. The patient planned to fill that bucket with poisonous scorpions.

'What nonsense,' my father had said. 'How is that efficient? You'd have to feed the scorpions, and when they eventually fell on you, it would be impossible to guarantee they'd actually sting you and if they did, how long that would take.' My father had advised him to schedule all his daily activities into timed slots, so that he could have more control over his life, which would result in him feeling better about himself.

I often sat on a bench in the park to watch the tourists climbing the steps of the Eiffel Tower. I wondered if it was easy to jump off it. According to my landlady, it was. You have to really want to do it, she said. She'd seen it happen three times. After that she stopped watching, she said, because it was a form of attention-seeking. But now she was in a hurry, so that was all she could tell me.

Each week I would knock on my landlady's door to pay the rent, and she always seemed to be on the way out. The first time I knocked was the only time she ever invited me inside. She lived in an apartment with herringbone parquet, Louis XVI furniture, and velvet curtains held back by golden cords. The former president, Giscard d'Estaing, was on the television. He was a friend of hers. 'I just want to watch this,' she said and motioned for me to sit next to her on the couch. The former president was stepping out of a black car and climbing the steps of a government building. A hair was sticking through my landlady's flesh-coloured pantyhose. Her feet were clad in red slippers. I smoothed the wrinkles out of my jeans and thought about hamburgers. I'd seen a Burger King on my way home from the metro station. The news report continued, and it seemed as if the woman had forgotten I was sitting there. I became nervous and started thinking about sex and about the writer, and then I thought about my French teacher.

After a few weeks of walking through Paris I was exhausted, and spending all my time alone was stressing me out. I monitored and evaluated every little movement I made. My shoes weren't elegant enough, and I tended to favour my heels when I walked, which gave me back pain. In cafés, I hesitated when ordering coffee, and was reticent in every social situation, so I never fell into conversation with anyone, except for the men who preyed on young girls and would only slink away if you shouted at them to leave you alone. I also spent far too much time lying in bed, my head was too small for my body, and I put too much mayonnaise on everything I ate. Meanwhile, I wasn't doing any writing.

'To be or not to be?' the writer once asked me. 'Which do you choose?'

I hesitated.

'Come on,' he said, 'you must know the answer.'

'To be,' I said eventually.

'No, silly, it's not to be.'

I didn't know why it was better not to be, and even though I had resolved not to call the writer from Paris, I ended up calling him to ask. He sounded surprised. When I asked how things were going, he told me that he'd just come back from a week in Normandy where he'd slept in an old hotel where they were practically the only guests. It reminded him of the hotel in *The Shining*, but without the blood in the lift.

'Were you with her?' I asked.

'Yes, of course I was with her.'

I heard myself asking if he had taken the butt plug with him and whether she'd liked it. Then I said that he obviously didn't do that kind of thing with her because she had carried his child, which made her sacred to him. He would always choose her, I continued, also because she had her driver's licence, and he could keep on teaching me about freedom, independence and the art of living, but in the end, he was just a stupid prick.

After that, I called my father. He understood why I felt so lost and advised me to schedule my daily activities into time slots.

'It will give you the feeling that everything is manageable.' He often used the words 'manageable' and 'functioning'. The people who came to see him could no longer function, and he made sure their lives were manageable again. He said that he thought I was brave, living alone in Paris at eighteen years old. 'It's not that far away from home,' I said, 'and I'm not that brave.'

I followed my father's advice. In the mornings I would write for three hours, with a ten-minute break after every hour during which I could, for example, paint my nails or go to the toilet, it was entirely up to me. In the afternoons I would walk with my notebook in my bag, exploring a different arrondissement each day, in ascending order. At weekends I was free.

The first few days went well. It didn't matter that I still didn't write very much. I walked through the Jardin des Tuileries and Les Halles, through the canopied shopping arcades in the second arrondissement, and around the impressive library building. To prevent back pain, I paid attention to the way I walked, rolling my feet correctly from heel to toe. Whenever I sat on a bench to rest, I'd take notes. Men would often come along and sit beside me. One of them wanted to know if I'd ever sucked a French dick, but most of them just wondered if I'd like to get a cup of coffee and why I wasn't very friendly.

At night I lay satisfied in bed. My father was right. I'd wanted to tell him that when he called, but he had just installed a new operating system on his computer and now nothing was working, even his card games had disappeared. In a panic, he listed all the buttons he'd pressed.

One night I slept badly, which meant that I stayed in bed

longer and started work later than usual, which also meant that I would eat lunch later and this distracted me because I was already hungry. And so, my father's cure stopped working. After lunch I fell asleep and dreamt that I missed my flight because I had too much luggage and couldn't choose which clothes to leave at home. You never know what kind of situation you'll find yourself in while in another country. Anxious, I threw the beautiful dress I'd just bought out of my suitcase. On the way to the airport, I realised what I'd done and decided to buy a new one before my flight. I visited all the airport shops at breakneck speed, but the wheels of my suitcase kept getting caught on every threshold.

'If you accidentally deviate from your schedule one day, try not to make up for lost time,' my father had advised. 'Instead, just try to carry on from where you left off the following day. Otherwise, you'll mess up your entire schedule.' But that evening I did try to salvage what I could of the day's writing. I'd been quite pleased with my last productive day. In the morning I'd written exactly one paragraph, and in the afternoon, I'd bought a dress on the Rue de Rennes and after that, I'd gone to a cinema in Odéon to see a pretty graphic serial killer movie about a psychopath who ate people. Before the film I'd sat on a bench and made some notes. The following night, I had opened my notebook to read them. *She sank into silent musings*, was the only thing I'd written underneath a couple of messy drawings of a woman with a sleepy face.

○

I decided to put the writing aside for a bit, because I had to see more of the world first. There were still several arrondissements I hadn't explored.

At night I thought about the writer in the empty hotel in Normandy and pictured him walking through a deserted hallway into a monumental dining room with chandeliers and a panoramic view of the sea, while laughing at everything his girlfriend said. I suspected that he didn't find the distance between her eyes too narrow. When I thought about the rumpled sheets in their hotel bed and the bathtub that was probably just big enough for two, I got angry, and also because I kept thinking about these kinds of things when he probably wasn't spending a single second thinking about me. To calm myself I tried to remember the names of all the psychopath's victims in the film. When I was younger, I used to listen to old recordings of my father's therapy sessions when I couldn't sleep. He'd given the cassettes to me so I could tape music over them. Most of the dialogue sounded like soothing murmurs, but sometimes I could make out fragments of the conversation. 'Why do you think you find that so difficult?' I once heard my father asking. One night, I suddenly woke to the sound of a strange man sobbing about being tired of everything. So tired.

After abandoning my writing schedule, I used the mornings to catch up on the sleep I missed at night. Sometimes I'd even nap in the afternoons, or in the evenings after dinner. Between all the sleeping, I attempted to see something of the world.

I hung over the railing of a bridge in the twelfth arrondissement and threw pieces of bread on the train tracks at Gare de Lyon, then watched the birds go after the bread, narrowly avoiding any oncoming trains. I tore one of my toenails in the sixteenth arrondissement when I caught my sandal on a paving stone while walking along the wide, clean footpath. One drizzly day, I was at the Sacre Coeur in the eighteenth arrondissement when a boy threw his boombox from the very top of the steps. The music only stopped when the radio was halfway down.

In the twentieth arrondissement I bought a cobalt blue silk scarf from a man with rust-coloured teeth at Belleville market. Then I wandered into a side street. It was quiet compared to the busy market. The streets in that neighbourhood were long and grey, and there seemed to be only young men walking around. Some of them hissed at me. I wrapped my new scarf around my shoulders and kept walking. When I noticed the same group of men I'd just passed, I realised that I'd been walking in a circle.

'Sweetheart, where are you going? Come here,' the men called after me, laughing at my angry expression. When I turned another corner, I thought I could see a metro station in the distance. I wanted to accelerate my pace (it had been quite some time since I'd paid any attention to the way my feet fell) when a boy who looked about ten approached me.

'Madame,' he said, 'where are you from?' Reluctantly, maybe because he used the word 'madame', I stopped.

'I'm from the Netherlands,' I said.

The boy told me about the window display at his uncle's jewellery shop, where the merchandise was touted in various languages. 'It's for the tourists,' he explained.

I looked at the phone shops in the street behind me.

'The tourists who visit the market,' he said. 'It's just around the corner.' He pointed in the direction I'd come from and asked if I would be interested in helping his uncle translate a few of his signs into Dutch. 'Please,' said the boy, 'it's close by.'

I decided to follow him. After a few moments I heard the bustle of the market and could relax again. The boy walked into a little laneway that took us to the boulevard, where the market sellers were shouting to get the attention of the customers, who were mostly women wearing hijabs. The shop window was decorated with colourful Christmas lights. Beside each piece of jewellery was a piece of cardboard bearing an English description. *Beautifull necklace, real stones naturel,* was written beside a necklace with gemstone pendants, and next to a ring: *Very old ring from Tunésie.*

Inside the shop, a portly North African man with greying hair was sitting on a stool behind a counter.

'Hello!' He pushed a stool towards me and motioned for me to sit. The boy disappeared through a door at the back of the shop. I smiled and hesitated beside a rack full of bracelets.

'Sit,' he said, and so I sat. The boy returned with a pot of tea and two glasses.

'No, no,' I said. 'I can't stay long.' My glass was filled with tea.

'My name is Mourad,' said the man, and he asked for my name and what I was doing in Paris. He nodded encouragingly at every answer I gave. When I started talking about my novel, he clapped his hands and said, 'A writer! What is your book about?' I explained that the story was still in the development phase, but it was primarily about a girl who moves to Paris to write a novel but spends most of her time sleeping, fretting and dealing with back pain.

'Nothing actually happens,' I said. 'She writes nothing and meets no one.'

We chatted for a while about Paris and back pain, and because he listened so attentively, I also told Mourad about the writer in the Netherlands who didn't want to have to choose, but who had actually chosen long ago. 'Even though his girlfriend is cross-eyed,' I said. And because he asked, I also told him about my mother, who was dead, and my father, who played solitaire when he came home from the insane asylum. I tried to explain about the suicide machine that my father's depressed patient had designed, but I couldn't find the right words. 'Never mind,' I said, and wondered if it would be impolite to leave.

'You're lonely,' said Mourad, and suddenly I started crying uncontrollably. Shrugging and hiccupping, I tried to regain control of my emotions.

'Relax,' he said forcefully as I attempted to stand. 'Let me help you.' He said he could feel how much grief I was carrying. After all the shrugging and hiccupping I felt dizzy and light in the head, as if I'd just smoked a fat joint. Mourad came and stood behind me and kneaded my shoulders.

'You're so tense,' he murmured.

Apparently, he was also a professional masseuse. His framed diploma was hanging on the wall. Mourad expertly massaged my shoulders and upper arms, then moved his hands down my back to my hips.

'Okay, thank you for everything,' I told him. 'But I have to go.'

'I'm not going to hurt you, you know. What kind of man do you think I am? This is my profession, I just want to help you get rid of your back pain. You're helping me and I'm helping you too.' He did his very best, massaging my hips and putting his hands under my shirt to run his hands up my spine. Then he suggested we go upstairs, where I could lie down for a bit. 'And I can do your legs.'

In a mezzanine in the space behind the shop, there was a grimy mattress on the floor. He grabbed my feet and massaged his way up my legs. My head began to hurt. He rubbed my groin with his thumbs. They touched the edges of my underpants and occasionally ventured just inside them.

'Okay, thank you,' I said and pulled my skirt down over my knees.

Downstairs, the boy had cut a cardboard box into small cards. 'Prachtige kettingen met echte natuursteen', I wrote in Dutch, and 'Antieke ring uit Tunesië'.

On my way home I bought two Whoppers and a large french fries at Burger King.

'I'm done,' I told my father that night when he asked how it was going. 'I've visited every arrondissement.'

The Best Years of My Bum

My father said: 'Yesterday was fun.' He sounded surprised. We had eaten at an expensive restaurant. I chose the place, he paid for it.

Now we were driving around the Place de la Concorde and cars were zipping past us. 'Bye, Paris,' I said.

My father beeped the horn and cut in front of another car. 'Bye, Paris!' he yelled.

It was entirely possible he was still drunk. Last night he'd told me four times that I still had my whole life ahead of me. The first time he mentioned it was when I started talking about the novel I'd planned to write while in Paris, which I'd never started. The second time was a little awkward, after I told him about the Dutch writer I'd fallen in love with who hadn't ended up choosing me. The third time was when I ordered duck roasted in duck fat without any vegetables — he'd actually said: 'You have the rest of your life to eat healthily' — and the last time he said it was at the end of the night, when I got drunk and started talking about the writer again.

My father still had a week before he had to return to work. He wanted to drive slowly north, via the coast, and had already booked hotels and restaurants along the way.

'I thought you wanted to take it slowly,' I said as we tore along Boulevard Périphérique. We'd left later than intended, and we had a lunch reservation.

There was a lot of traffic, and my father was really stepping hard on the accelerator. Every time a car drove too slowly in front of us, he'd brake with a sudden jerk. I was nauseated before we even left Paris.

We arrived at our first hotel just in time for lunch. The building had wooden balconies and was located opposite the Deauville marina. We ordered fish. My father shoved almost all of the tail in his mouth at once. Tiny white pieces of fish got caught in his beard.

That night we went to the casino by the beach. My father exchanged three hundred francs and gave me half the chips.

'Don't spend it all at once,' he said. I put fifteen francs on red at the roulette table and won. Then I put everything on red and lost. My father was standing on the other side of the room, pulling on the handle of a slot machine. From this angle, you couldn't see his belly, and he looked just like one of the guys from the Cannabis Café where I used to work, except that none of them wore corduroy.

I walked into the poker room. Lots of large men in tight sweaters were sitting around the tables. I went over to the table with the biggest crowd around it. The players were all focussed on their cards. Some of them were sweating profusely. Sitting beside the man with the tallest pile of chips was a heavily made-up woman, wearing a dress with a neckline cut all the way down to her navel. She was watching with a sullen expression on her face. That woman should swallow some of her make-up, I thought, so she can be equally beautiful on the inside. I'd once heard a rich American woman with silicone boobs say this about another rich American woman with silicone boobs on TV. The boobs of the woman at the poker table were sagging. Apart from that not much was happening. I walked over to a different table, which had no audience. A couple of the players looked up when I came to stand beside them.

'Sorry,' I mumbled.

'Pardon?' said the dealer. 'You're not allowed to whisper.'

'Oh, sorry,' I said, more loudly.

In the meantime, my father had come into the poker room and was waving his hands at me. He looked a little overheated. When he started trying to sign letters with his fingers, a security guard walked over and escorted him out of the room.

'I won,' he said, when we were eventually reunited by

the slot machines. 'Thirty-nine hundred francs, thirteen hundred guilders.'

He'd fed just seven hundred and fifty francs into the machine, the exact amount he'd taken out of the ATM to pay our hotel bill. When we got back to the hotel, we celebrated by each taking three drinks from the minibar.

The following day I only felt nauseated once we arrived in Dieppe. Some of the traffic lights were crooked, and hidden behind the road signs, and I almost hit my head on the dashboard every time my father noticed one. 'Dieppe is famous for its coquilles and the Allied landing in 1942, which didn't end so well,' said my father, who was always fully primed for his holidays. He'd reserved another hotel at a marina. 'At seven-thirty, we're booked in to eat coquilles Saint Jacques at a restaurant on the boulevard,' he said as he handed me my room key.

'So, what do you think of them?' he asked eagerly.

'They're okay,' I said.

'These are the best coquilles Saint Jacques in all of France.' My father only made that kind of sweeping statement when he had no real knowledge of the topic at hand. When it came to topics he was familiar with, he could relativise until there was nothing left to discuss. I wondered sometimes if he was this long-winded with his patients. He spoke so softly on his tapes that it was often difficult to understand him. A therapist shouldn't speak too much, I thought, even if they're speaking softly, but I wasn't entirely sure. I had very little experience as a patient. We had seen a family therapist for a while, back when my mother was always angry and my father was depressed. But it had been an alternative form of therapy, because my mother didn't want my father using his professional knowledge to his advantage.

We were told to act as though some dolls were the members of our family. The idea was to give our emotions free rein. My father and I first had to get over our trepidation, but afterwards we did feel quite liberated. During our second session, I managed to punch a hole in the mother doll's stomach and slam the father doll's head against the wall. I'm not sure exactly what my father did, but according to our therapist the two of us had shown more aggression than he'd he expected. After only a few weeks of therapy, he suggested that we stop seeing him altogether.

'Incidentally, Dieppe is also very important for the banana,' said my father. He'd managed to stuff an entire coquille into the pouch of his cheek. 'The bananas that came through the port here were distributed throughout all of France.'

After dinner, I collected stones on the beach and threw them as far out to sea as I could.

'That's a nice bum you've got there,' said a man with a weathered face who was collecting empty bottles. It wasn't the first time someone had said something like that to me. My mother used to have the same kind of bum: large and firm. Though, in her later years it was more of a pancake. I approached a colony of gulls and they took off in one fluid movement. These are my bum's best years, I thought wistfully, and I'm wasting them.

The next stop on our journey was Saint-Valéry-sur-Somme, which my father had chosen because of the seals. They lived in a bay close to the village.

'We'll take the steam train tomorrow and go right past them,' he said. 'Isn't that extraordinary?'

Saint-Valéry-sur-Somme was full of elderly tourists who wore raincoats and used walking sticks. In the hotel dining room, they ground white fish to pulp between their dentures. My father was in the mood for steak. Pieces of gristle and fat kept getting stuck between his teeth, but he wasn't able to get them out with his tongue, so he stuck almost his entire hand in his mouth. Once his fingers finally managed to latch onto a meaty thread caught between two back teeth, he started frantically tugging on it.

He's spending too much time alone, I thought. He needs a new wife, maybe one of the nice social workers from the insitution. They were often upbeat, practical women, who wouldn't shout at him if he happened to drop a cup, even if it was one of the antique coffee cups from the display cabinet in his living room.

'Please stop,' I said. 'You look like one of the severely disturbed people from your work.'

The following day the steam train was half filled with passengers, and most of them had grey hair. My father and I sat in the front carriage, by a window. There were enormous sweat stains under his arms. It had taken us some time to locate the train's departure point, but eventually we were the first to board, because my father had pushed in front of a couple using walking sticks. I'd yelled at him, and was now feeling guilty.

'Look, they have a menu.' I tried to sound upbeat while pointing at the plastic-covered menu on our table.

'Uhuh,' said my father, sounding tired. He always sounded tired when he was feeling sorry for himself.

Outside, an old man was helping his elderly wife onto the running board, and I imagined him climbing into bed with her. This made me think of the writer again. Then I thought about the seventy-year-old man I'd seen on television, who would masturbate for hours when his wife wasn't around. He said he liked to do it in the garden, and always delayed his orgasms, sometimes for an entire week, because it made them extra intense. For a moment, I thought about my father being at home without my mother, then quickly turned my thoughts to the seals we were about to see.

In the meantime, the train had started moving. My father pointed at the white birds in the bay.

'Spoonbills,' he said, as I nodded and looked. 'A horse,' he said a little later, and I looked at the horse. We went on like this for a while, past a sheep and another horse, until we reached the seals. All the pensioners stood up to take photos. My father did too. He went and stood in the aisle so he could include me in the photos.

'Come on, smile,' he said.

The engine started making strange noises on the highway to Dunkirk. My father stopped in the emergency lane and bent over the engine for a long time. When he got back behind the wheel, the car wouldn't start.

'We have to get to a mechanic,' he said, sounding tired.

We were picked up by a tow truck. The driver, a man with large jowls and cold, piercing eyes, used a chain to hoist our car onto the back of his truck, then asked us to get in. There wasn't any room up front in the cab with him, he said. The passenger's seat was out of commission.

'Why?' I asked. It needed to be reupholstered. The driver stared at me long and hard when he said this. If I disregarded his nose and forehead, he looked just like John Wayne Gacy, an American contractor who'd dressed up as a clown and performed at children's parties in his spare time. I'd just read a book about the thirty-three boys he'd raped, tortured and murdered in the seventies. Gacy would often begin with his handcuff trick — telling the boys he could free them from handcuffs without using a key — and he liked to finish with his rope trick, which consisted of him tying a rope around his victim's neck and tightening the knot until they choked to death.

'Why would the seat need to be reupholstered?' I asked

my father as we sat in our car on top of the tow truck. I handed him a roll of peppermints.

'Maybe he spilled coffee over it,' said my father, sliding his peppermint from one cheek to the other and back again.

'He isn't the type of man to worry about coffee stains,' I said. 'Did you see those eyes? He's probably a psychopath.'

My father sighed. 'It's not that simple,' he began. 'There are many different forms of psychopathy. And within each sub-category there are so many variations, which are also dependent on other factors. For example, a person's environment can determine whether any latent psychopathic tendencies continue to develop or not.'

'Can't you just chew on that peppermint, then swallow it?!'

He took the mint out of his mouth and threw it out the window.

'You've always been so aggressive.'

'You know who was actually aggressive?' I said. 'Mama.'

'Your mother was expressive.'

'No, she was always angry, and you didn't even notice. She was jealous too. If anyone ever gave you a compliment, she'd put you down in front of everyone. Have you forgotten that?'

'Oh, come on,' he said. 'It wasn't that bad. And anyway, I was talking about you.'

'No,' I said, 'we're talking about you. You're completely deluded, and you drive like a maniac. That's why the engine isn't working.'

The tow truck exited the highway and made a sharp turn. I had to steady myself to keep from sliding into my father. I glanced over at him. His cheek was pressed against the window, he looked defeated, and his fingers were clenched around the door handle.

We had to wait two days for the car to be repaired in a village without a marina, beach or any local delicacies. The tow truck driver, who also owned the garage, had brought us to a hotel on the village square. The building was quite dilapidated and had a bar on the ground floor with one slot machine. A guy in a worn-out Metallica shirt was playing the machine. The barman, who was also the owner of the hotel, checked us in. He had the same jowls as the garage owner, but his eyes were weaker. The barman pointed listlessly at the swinging door. Behind it was a hallway that led to a terrace and the stairs we had to take to our rooms.

'Merci hè!' my father exclaimed. He always sounded jovial when he spoke French.

The rooms had no minibar. I opened the window, lay down on the musty-smelling bed, and closed my eyes. The writer once told me that his favourite thing to do while abroad was lie in bed in his hotel room with the windows open. He didn't feel compelled to experience anything else. Outside, a scooter alarm was going off, and I could hear my father on the phone with the garage owner in the room next door. I wondered if the garage owner had a wife and family, and if his wife found it difficult to deal with his psychopathic tendencies, or if she just turned a blind eye to it.

'Once they reach a certain age, women want a family more than anything,' the writer said. 'Then they're not as picky as they once were.' He didn't necessarily want a family, which is why he lived at his own place during the week. Up high in his flat and alone, with a book in his lap and the windows open.

My father had wanted a family, but once I arrived, he had a nervous breakdown. One night, after drinking a bottle of jenever, he'd snuck into the garage, pushed the car onto the street, then driven away. According to my mother, he wanted to die, but he still denies this. He just wanted to go, to leave the world behind. Somewhere just outside the city, he'd lost control of the car while turning a corner and ended up driving through some barbed wire into a field. Tsk, tsk. The sound of the barbed wire scraping across the roof of the car was something he never forgot.

'After that, whenever he found himself in that kind of mood,' said my mother, 'I'd go and sit on the floor in front of the garage door so he couldn't get the car out.' She had sat there for a few nights, but he'd never needed to leave again.

'Shall we go and get something to eat?' my father yelled. I was woken by the sound of his wedding ring tapping against my door. The hotel restaurant had a small patio on the courtyard: four plastic tables with outdoor chairs under a canopy. We were the only guests. An electric bug zapper on the wall emitted a blueish light. We ate sausages with fries, my father drank loads of wine and kept filling my glass too. We had no plans for the following day anyway.

'The car problems have put us two days behind schedule,' he said. 'So, we'll have to drive straight home the day after tomorrow.' He explained in detail the route we'd have to take and then started talking about the head gasket sealing the engine and what happens when it catches fire. The bug zapper crackled when a fly flew into it. Still two nights to go, I thought.

After dessert, the bartender brought out a bottle of eau de vie.

'Listen,' said my father, making two attempts to pick up his glass, 'I think you're doing so well.'

'What am I doing well?'

'Everything.'

His eyes looked watery, but it was hard to see properly in the blue light.

'And as for the affair with the married man …'

'He isn't married,' I said quickly. 'He doesn't even live with his girlfriend. And it wasn't just an affair, it was true love.'

'Fine, but he does have a girlfriend and a child,' said my father. 'He's bound to someone else.'

While he insisted that it wasn't my fault because he'd been absent for years after my mother's death, and probably also in the years preceding that, but now he was really going to pay more attention to me, the word 'bound' got stuck in my mind. The writer wasn't free at all, he was bound to someone else. He hadn't made a choice, he'd been trapped.

'I think you're *thrilling*,' he'd once told me. I only ever knew him to be drunk, stoned or high on coke. I thought about his old bike and how I'd like to slit the tyres.

'Did you feel trapped when you missed the turn and drove the car through the barbed wire into the field?'

'Oh,' said my father, 'it's not so bad being bound to someone, but you need to be able to remain functional.'

'Yeah,' I said. 'You weren't functioning.'

He filled my glass again.

'You know, freedom really isn't so great. In the end, all it means is that you're sitting at home alone.'

My father was snoring in the other room. A dog barked outside. I got dressed in the dark and walked downstairs to the bar. Some of the regulars were still sitting there, drinking. The guy in the Metallica shirt was standing at the slot machine. I ordered a glass of wine and went to sit at a small table by the window. The guy didn't look up or acknowledge me. He had wild curly hair and a big nose, like Bob Dylan, but was slightly better looking. My hairdresser thinks that if you have a big nose, it's best to get a haircut that reveals as much of your face as possible. I camouflaged my nose by plucking my eyebrows into arches because my hairdresser said it would balance out my face. This guy's eyebrows were hidden under his thick, bushy curls. He pulled on the slot machine's handle the same way my father pulled on the gear stick: furiously, almost panicked. I wondered if he'd been standing there the whole day, or if he'd taken a break to go home and eat.

He had gone home for dinner, he said when he came over to change some money while I was standing at the bar. His mother had made ragout with potatoes. He looked awkwardly past me at the slot machine. No, he hadn't won anything yet, but he had managed to win three hundred and fifty francs the previous week, so it could still turn in his favour. The eyes beneath that frizzy fringe seemed reasonably intelligent.

Jean-Marie was his name. He continued pulling on the lever while giving short answers to my questions. Metallica was his favourite band but he'd never seen them in concert. And he'd been to Paris only once, with his uncle.

'For business,' he said. He'd had to repeat that a couple of times before I understood that he was speaking in English. No, he hadn't been to the top of the Eiffel Tower, but he had asked his uncle to drive past it on their way to the world's largest scrapyard, which was near the Bois de Vincennes. I happened to know that there were also a lot of sex workers in that area, including male sex workers, who stood on the side of the road with their dicks hanging out. He tore his eyes away from the slot machine for a moment.

'I wouldn't know anything about that,' he said.

'Now you'll know for the next time you go,' I said.

Jean-Marie wanted to be an engineer, but for now, he was working for his uncle at the garage.

'Is that your uncle!' I shrieked. I asked about the passenger seat in his tow truck, but Jean-Marie had no idea what had happened. 'That's strange,' I said. His uncle had a wife and two kids and, as far as Jean-Marie knew, he wasn't a pathological liar, but they generally only spoke about cars. And no, he wasn't completely lacking in empathy because he'd recently told Jean-Marie he felt sorry for the hotel owner because he had such an ugly wife. Jean-Marie laughed. I listed a few other psychopathic personality traits, but Jean-Marie swore and gave the slot machine a shove. He'd put his last few francs into the machine but hadn't won the jackpot.

'Come,' I said. On a bench in the village square, Jean-Marie stuck his tongue in my mouth and felt my boobs. I rubbed his erection through his pants.

'Come,' said Jean-Marie after a while. And on a flower bed between some bushes, he came on my stomach, then wiped me clean with his Metallica shirt.

'You're all right,' he said.

I nodded. And that was that, I thought. Now I'm over the writer.

'We don't have anything scheduled for today,' my father said the following morning, before tearing a croissant in half with his teeth. 'I'm going to head over to the garage this afternoon, and maybe we could check out the church before that.'

The church on the square was closed. We looked at it from the outside, then walked along the sole high street to the edge of the village, where we found an abandoned tennis court behind a tall fence. There were huge holes in the fence, and large branches and empty beer cans lying on the concrete court. My father walked onto the court, picked up the cans, and threw them in the bin. The bin had metal rings on either side so that the local council's trucks could pick it up and empty it. My father stuck his hand through one of the rings.

'Just trying it on.' This was a phrase coined by one of his patients who compulsively stuck his hand into any available hole, including open windows, toilets or yawning mouths. It fit him. My father and I looked at the metal ring around his wrist, and then he checked his watch.

'We have to go,' he said. 'I have to get to the garage.' He tried to pull his hand out of the ring, but it got stuck. He kept trying, pulling his arm harder and harder.

'Why don't you crouch down, then hold your arm up above you, so all the blood drains out of it.'

My father got on his haunches, and for a moment, he reminded me of our dog. At the end of his life, the dog had been so weak that he kept falling into his own turds whenever he tried to do a poop. My father had cried when he died. It was only the second time I'd seen him cry. The first time was when my mother died. Both the dog and my mother had cancer and passed peacefully in their sleep. My father and I had driven to the vet together. The dog sat on his lap because my father insisted on holding him. Wrapped in a blanket, the animal had nestled into my father's chest, with its head on my father's shoulder. We encountered three stoplights and one slow driver along the way. Every time my father hit the brakes, the dog would whimper, and my father would whisper calming words in his ear. 'Calm down, sweetheart,' he said, like he used to say to my mother. On our way back from the vet, without the dog, we let ourselves slump forward in our seats at every stoplight.

My father was now tugging wildly at the metal ring. Sometimes people get so stuck they have to break their own limbs to free themselves. Films are made about people who do that kind of thing. I wondered how to go about breaking a thumb. You'd probably have to pull it quite hard. I felt tears welling up, but I had to stay strong. 'Go back to the hotel,' said my father, 'and ask them to call the fire brigade. They'll have to saw me out of this.'

The hotel owner shrugged.

'The closest fire brigade is thirty kilometres away.'

'Is there someone else who could help?' I asked.

'Why would anyone stick their hand through one of those rings?' he asked, before turning to pick up his telephone. 'The garage owner is on his way.'

The garage owner was also the local handyman. His

truck was fully loaded, with two cars on the back of it, and the passenger seat had been repaired. Jean-Marie was sitting next to him, wearing a plain grey shirt covered in black smudges. And on his big nose, beneath the frizzy hair, he was sporting a fire-engine red pimple.

The garage owner looked first at me and then at my father, who was trying to casually lean on the plastic bin cover with his free hand.

'I could saw through that ring in no time,' he said after a short pause, 'but your hand would have to come off too.'

'Maybe we could break his thumb,' I suggested 'and slide his hand out.'

They all stared at me.

'Good idea,' said the garage owner. He bent over my father's hand. 'Or we could break the rest of the bones in his body and pull his entire body through the ring.' He squinted when he laughed, which made him look like a heavier version of Hitler. He retrieved a bottle of lube oil from the front of the tow truck. 'This should do the trick.'

Jean-Marie went and sat in the driver's seat of the truck. I got in beside him. We watched through the grimy windscreen as my father twisted his arm and tried to slide his hand back through the ring. Every so often, the garage owner would pour more lube over his hand. This is going to take a while, I thought, and opened the glove box.

'What are you doing?' asked Jean-Marie.

'Stop breathing down my neck,' I said. Inside the glove box, there were some registration papers, an open packet of latex gloves and a crumpled McDonald's bag. I searched for traces of blood on the cardboard box full of gloves, but there weren't any. Meanwhile, my father was pushing down on the ring with the entire weight of his body. The garage owner fiddled with his fingers. Then, there was a loud scream. My father fell backwards, clutching one hand with the other.

'Goddamn it,' he said. 'My thumb.'

'Jesus!' I cried, running over and crouching down beside him. 'Papa.'

The garage owner was already back beside his tow truck. 'Come on,' he said, waving at one of the cars on the back of his truck. 'Hop in.'

My father attempted to stand. He winced in pain, and I noticed a little sliver of his breakfast croissant stuck to one of his incisors.

'Everything is fine, darling,' he said firmly. But everything wasn't fine. It hadn't been fine for a long time, and suddenly, I wasn't sure how to keep going.

Party

'It's time to say goodbye,' said my mother, 'because I'm going to die.' She was sitting in bed wearing a peach-coloured balconette bra with little bows on the straps. Her breasts were bulging, her cheeks were black with mascara and I was on my knees beside her bed. Through a gap in the sheets, I could see part of her garter belt and a few dimples on her thigh.

'Are you really going to die?' I asked her tearfully. She nodded. I looked at the babysitter. She also nodded. My father had run downstairs to let the doctor in. The last time I'd seen him panic like this was the afternoon I went missing. While walking the dog, I'd met a man who wanted to show me his fountain. 'It's a very old fountain,' he said, and then he asked my age. 'I'm eight,' I said. 'That's also old.'

In his garden, there was a marble fountain with a large statue of a laughing Buddha at the top of it. Water trickled from Buddha's folded hands into the shell-shaped basin below. The man explained that the fountain came from an Indian palace. Princes and princesses had sat on the edge of that basin and dipped their hands in the water. I went and sat on the edge of the basin and watched as my dog stuck his tongue in the water then started to slobber.

'Let's not do that,' said the man, giving the dog a shove with his foot. 'Do you know what will bring you luck? Rubbing Buddha's belly with your hand.' I bent over and gave Buddha's glistening belly several vigorous rubs. The man bent over me and stroked my hair and my back, which I found a little uncomfortable. Maybe he doesn't have any children of his own, I thought, and waited until he was done.

When the dog stuck his tongue in the fountain again, the man said it was best I went home, but I was welcome to come back anytime without the dog. When I got home, my father was on the phone and had huge sweat stains coming from his armpits. He pulled me into his arms as soon as he saw me.

My parents had gone to a party, and the sitter and I were braiding each other's hair. She had thick brown hair that I constantly wanted to touch because it was so smooth. Her lips were a beautiful shade of red, and she wore glitter from a tube on her cheeks. She let me put some on my face too. Then things got a bit awkward when she started applying my lipstick. Whenever I got nervous or found myself in a situation where I felt trapped with other people, I'd do the most awful farts. As soon as I remembered this, it happened.

'How can such a small child stink so badly?' my mother often asked. No one knew the answer. Sometimes I was able to hold in my farts by clenching my bum cheeks together. But this time it hadn't worked. I bowed my head in shame, which made the sitter's hand slip, then she had to get a kitchen cloth to wipe the red stripe of lipstick off my forehead. I held her nose while she cleaned me.

Later that night I woke to the sound of the front door. I heard my mother talking loudly. 'There's something there,' she kept saying. When I came downstairs, I found my father trying to wrestle a kitchen knife out of my mother's hands. The dog stood beside them, wagging his tail, and the sitter was watching it all, with her shoulders hunched.

'What's going on?' I asked.

'There's something in my head,' said my mother 'and it has to be removed.' She sounded determined. 'Maybe it'll be easier with a bottle opener.'

My father went and stood in front of the cutlery drawer.

'Papa, what's wrong with her?' I asked him in shock. He was sure to know.

'I don't know,' he said. Very carefully, he pushed her up the stairs and into their room, where she collapsed on the bed and just lay there.

'Talk to her, Papa,' I said, because I knew that's how he healed people. And those people were truly crazy, they stuck vegetable peelers down their throats or touched their penis whenever they saw a little girl. He would tell us about them during dinner. But now it seemed as if my father couldn't think of what to do.

'You stay here with her,' he said to the sitter. 'I'm going to call the doctor.' Then he went back downstairs.

So, I'll have to do it, I decided, because the sitter was just standing there like a sack of potatoes. I got on my knees beside my mother's bed. 'Can you tell me what's going on?' I asked her softly.

She gave me an intense look.

'Yes,' she said. 'You have stars on your cheeks.' She drew circles on my cheek with her finger.

'It's glitter,' I said, but my mother had stopped listening. She looked at her hands in surprise and then held them up in front of her.

'These aren't my hands,' she said. 'These are Aunt Ibby's hands. What are these old hands doing here?' Suddenly, she spread her arms wide, almost hitting me in the face.

As long as we can keep talking, I thought. It was raining softly outside.

'Oh, God,' my mother continued. 'Aunt Ibby is dying and that's why I have her hands. I'm sure that's it. Go and get your father.'

My mother insisted that my father call Aunt Ibby to ask how she was. But apart from her varicose veins and her hip that tended to hurt a bit when it rained like this, Ibby was fine and didn't feel like she was about to die.

'Then they must be my hands,' said my mother,

sounding gutted when my father hung up the phone. She wriggled out of her dress and got under the covers.

'Guys,' she said, 'I'm going to die.' Black mascara tears ran down her cheeks, and I started sobbing too.

'Oh, darling,' said my mother, 'I so wanted to see you grow up.'

I rubbed my eyes until they hurt. Through a haze of tears and glitter, I watched my mother as she leant back into the pillows.

'Don't die!' I shrieked and threw myself onto her bed. The sitter came to sit beside me and began softly stroking my back. Briefly, the man with the fountain crossed my mind, and I thought about his laughing Buddha that hadn't brought me any luck at all.

My mother was now staring at the ceiling with her hands folded over her belly.

'We'd better say our goodbyes,' she said again. Her voice was already weakening.

When my father walked in with the doctor, I was weeping, my snotty face pressed into my mother's lap. Behind me the sitter was also softly crying. Everything was covered in glitter, even my mother's black cheeks and décolleté.

'How's it going over here?' the doctor asked brightly. He bent and looked at my mother. 'What have you taken, Madame?'

'Nothing,' said my mother. 'Just some sherry.' She'd also eaten some cake and liverwurst. The cake had been dark brown, but, now the doctor was asking, the cake hadn't tasted very much like chocolate. 'And it didn't taste like blackberries either,' said my mother, who knew a thing or two about baking cakes.

'You're having a bad trip,' said the doctor. 'You need to drink a lot of water and get some sleep.'

'And then?' I asked with concern.

'Don't eat any more brown cake,' he said. The doctor laughed loudly at his own joke. My father and the sitter laughed too. I clenched my bum cheeks together.

Small Head

My best friend Thomas made me put my head under a guillotine. A rubber model of my head was then supposed to fall into a basket. Thomas was the assistant to a man who did special effects for film and TV shows. They were working on a film about the French Revolution.

The first time I saw Thomas was on the set of a crime film I was appearing in as a dead body.

'Oh!' I cried when he shook my hand. For a moment, I thought he'd wrapped his flaccid penis in a condom and put it in my hand. But when I looked down, I saw that it was actually a vinyl glove filled with maggots. He'd tied a knot in the top of the glove and hidden it in his sleeve. The maggots had come from the fishing supply shop, he said. They were going to be used on a body that had been decomposing in a luxury apartment building for a long time. Later, I would be discovered in the same neighbourhood. A fresh corpse with several large, gaping holes. Thomas had a book filled with photos of murdered people he used as inspiration for the wounds he made. I leafed through it while waiting for my scene, mostly so I knew what to do with my face while being a dead body. Some of them had their mouths wide open, and others looked like they were laughing, but most just looked blasé.

I lived in a storage room. The owner of the building had installed a kitchenette and a bathroom, which made the space habitable. My father thought it was quite spacious for a student. According to him, students were supposed to deny themselves any creature comforts because it would toughen them up. He often spoke about his student days, especially the night he'd been tarred and feathered by the older members of his fraternity, then paraded with the other first-year pledges through the streets with cracked raw eggs in his underwear. Some of the other pledges collapsed from tiredness and the cold along the way, and had to be picked up by their parents. But not him.

'The trick is just not to think,' he told me.

At night, I could hear animals scratching in the suspended ceiling. Mice, I thought initially, but they made so much noise that I started to think it was rats after all. One night there was a loud crash caused by one of them falling into the small space behind the plaster wall right next to my bed. At first, he tried to crawl his way back to the top but kept falling down, and then it seemed as if he was trying to chew his way through the wall, every single night.

In *The Painted Bird* by Jerzy Kosiński, the main protagonist watches as hungry rats gnaw their way through someone's body. My mother read that book when she was pregnant with me. I read it while she was dying. Whenever I found myself lying awake, worrying about things, I'd reread it. In particular, the passage about the Cossacks tearing out a farmer's eye and forcing him to eat it usually helped me to fall asleep, but after a few hours I'd wake again and my thoughts would race on, with the steady gnawing of the rat in the background.

Thomas also lived in a storage room, just a few streets away from mine. He kept a jar of sleeping pills he didn't use in the medicine cabinet above his toilet. I regularly thought about slipping the jar into one of the deep pockets of my pleated trousers. My mother once told me that you had to put a plastic bag over your head after taking those pills. A friend of hers had done it. The cleaner had found her with her mouth wide open, a bit like the bodies pictured in Thomas' book. My mother's friend had lost her husband a few months earlier to a neuromuscular disease. He'd been allowed to undergo euthanasia. Suicide under supervision seemed like a better option to me. I preferred fantasising about euthanasia.

I did my best to live. Thomas recommended a healer who was an eighty-year-old former CIA agent. The healer rang my doorbell one drizzly Thursday morning. He looked like a gnome, and when he went to sit on my couch, he fell so far back that his feet flew into the air. He'd never been in the CIA, he said a little later, my friend had misunderstood him. And he wasn't eighty, he was fifty-seven. The healer took a sip of tea and looked straight at me. Then he snatched the air a few times, as if trying to catch a fly.

'How are you feeling now?' he asked. I wondered if the session had already started or if I still had time to serve the biscuits I'd bought for him.

According to the gnome, I'd been an elf in a past life.

'Or a nymph,' he said, 'or a whale.' After a while he started talking about my father. He was certain that I'd known him in a former life, when we were both Japanese. We'd been in love, but because my family had a higher social standing than his, I'd been forced to marry someone else. My father had moved onto another woman and our paths diverged.

'He's always held onto the idea that he's not good enough for you. And you still feel like he's forgotten you.'

'But my father can't stand the Japanese,' I said. 'Because of the war.'

Thomas' mother had done a reiki course, and she told me I needed to ground myself. She bent her knees and began shaking her body. That was how you did it. Thomas and I copied her.

'You don't need to do it,' his mother told Thomas. 'You're already grounded.'

Thomas had been in a concentration camp in one of his former lives. He didn't remember anything about it, but when the gnome had told him this, he didn't find it such a crazy idea. After all, he had binge-watched the documentary *Shoah* in its entirety when his girlfriend broke up with him.

'Maybe I was also in a concentration camp,' I said, then told him about a dream that I'd had when I was four. I'd found myself standing on a gloomy field of grass with a group of people and been forced to point at someone. I'd cried while doing what I was told to do and then the person I'd pointed at was shot and killed.

'Maybe I was that person,' said Thomas. It didn't seem implausible to me.

My father thought I got caught up in other people's fantasies far too easily. I think he might have been right about that. There were just a lot of scenarios that I could imagine happening. My father said he could also see a lot of things happening, but that didn't mean he believed everything he was told.

'You're better off learning to trust your own intuition and reason,' he said on the telephone, sounding like he was in a hurry.

'Do you think I'm too much?' I asked. 'You hardly ever call me anymore.'

'I have a trial membership at a gym, darling, you know that.'

Everything is grey, I kept thinking. The balcony fence of the apartment behind mine was covered in pigeon shit. The guy who lived there had installed wire mesh panels between the fence and the ceiling, and every afternoon, he'd sit behind the wire on a plastic chair. Sometimes he grilled sausages on his barbeque. We'd exchange glances when I closed my window to keep the smoke from getting inside, but we never said hello.

Ever since his girlfriend had left him, Thomas also felt like everything was grey. In his twenty-four years on earth, he'd never been so in love. The first time he was invited to her place, she told him to bring a vintage bottle of single malt whisky. 'Balblair,' she said, 'it's the only one I'll accept.' Halfway through the bottle, she grabbed his face and bit him hard on the lip. While telling me this, he beamed and ran his tongue over the scar on the inside of his lower lip. In the months that followed, I only saw him when she had no time to see him. He developed dark circles under his eyes and was suddenly wearing jackets all the time. And he said things like: 'The big city is an alienating setting' and 'May I have a slice of lemon for my glass of water?'

This went on until she didn't know what she wanted anymore. She slept with someone else to try and figure it out, but that only confused her more. Maybe she needed to be alone for a while, she said. And after that she was alone for quite some time and it was all fine, except for when she went to visit him. The following day she would find herself confused all over again and then call him to tell him about it. He'd spend hours discussing it with her, then afterwards he'd analyse those discussions with me.

But there were times that I also wanted to tell him something. How my thesis was going, for example. My thesis wasn't going well at all. I'd been working on it for a whole year and hadn't even managed to write half of it. When I thought about it, my throat would close and my heart would start beating out of my chest, as if I were in imminent danger.

My computer sat on a round table in the middle of room, like a large grey pimple. Every morning, I'd smoke a cigarette, watch *The Oprah Winfrey Show*, eat a kiwi fruit, retch a few times, and then start doing my laps around the table. From the couch to the kitchen counter, from the counter to the toilet, from the toilet to the bed, and from the bed back to the couch. If I was able to get myself to sit at the computer and write a few lines, it was only a matter of time before I deleted them and the whole cycle would begin again. One of Oprah's guests said that people who found themselves stuck in similar cycles and wanted to make some changes should imagine how they wanted their lives to be and start acting as if they already had that life. He'd written several successful books on the subject. I imagined myself already graduated and dancing on top of a table in a bikini at a beach bar somewhere, just like I always saw people doing on MTV. But I wasn't feeling it. You have to really feel it, the successful writer said to Oprah.

Thomas thought I made an excellent corpse, because I was really good at lying still. But it didn't pay a living wage. My father paid the rent until I graduated. After that, I had to get a real job and pay him back.

When I was eight, my teacher asked me to write down what I wanted to be when I grew up. I wanted to be the person who wrote the script for the nightly news at seven, and if that wasn't possible, I'd want to be Tina Turner's backup singer. My father thought my ambitions were realistic. My mother frowned when she read them.

'Why not the lead singer?' she asked.

This startled me.

'I didn't really think about that,' I said. Later that night, in my room, I took a pen and crossed out the words *backup singer*.

According to my mother, my birth had been the reason her acting career had stalled. That and my father, whose work meant he wasn't home very often. Later, it was because of her illness. A teacher at her acting school had once said that she was the most talented of all the students that year.

'So, it had nothing to do my talent,' she liked to say. She believed it had nothing to do with my talent either. 'Write a book,' she would tell me if I came to her with a story.

A few years before I was born, she'd played the leading role in a television series that was cancelled after one season because not enough people had watched it. While she was sick, we often watched videos of her series. When the camera was on her she spoke differently. Too proper, I thought. But she looked beautiful, especially in close-up shots when she would gaze through her fringe into the middle distance. Her fringe was so thick it made me laugh.

'I'd rather be bald,' I once said, and she found that funny. Because we both knew that a bald head wouldn't suit me at all. I needed lots of hair to camouflage the fact that my head was too small for my body, which is why I was always teasing my ponytail. My mother was fortunate enough to have a large head. She looked good bald.

'Having a small head is actually quite handy when it comes to the guillotine,' said Thomas. We were sitting in his storage room. He'd put a shower cap on my head and smeared paste from the top of my head until it covered my entire face and ears. Over that, he put a plaster cast that was supposed to stay on for half an hour. I was given straws so I could breathe through my nose. Thomas nervously tapped on my cheek and forehead. 'Is it getting hard?' If this went well, his boss would let him work on bigger projects. He sighed and switched on the television. An MTV VJ was energetically reporting on a music event. It was the VJ with the platinum blonde hair, bright red full lips, and relatively large head. I recognised her voice.

'She's stopped answering the phone when I call,' said Thomas. He'd seen his ex-girlfriend sitting at an ice cream parlour with another man. The man's hand was on her thigh. 'On her thigh,' he repeated. The VJ was crowing something about a singer's extremely short dress. She wondered if the singer was even wearing any underwear.

Maybe it was a good thing, I thought, that he'd seen her with someone else. It was high time he forgot about her. One night after dinner, my mother told me that she had an admirer, a young man she met on the train. She'd gone to meet him in the city, and he had stroked her hands. Nothing else happened, she said. My father had been in the kitchen, and she giggled when he reappeared without warning, holding a carton of custard.

'It's not as if we're still in a relationship,' said Thomas. I shook my head slowly. In my opinion, the plaster had hardened. He stood up and got something out of the fridge. 'I still have her bracelet,' he said, and started talking about her good taste in things, her bossiness — sometimes she wouldn't let him talk or breathe in her direction — and her impulsivity, which he also found quite exciting. He would never have stolen that boat on his own.

I sniffed and fiddled with the straws in my nose. I never managed to get anything done on my own. While other people my age were out dancing on tables, I spent every evening staring at the suspended ceiling. There was no reason to think I wouldn't still be lying there in twenty years, when all the other adults had children that were almost adults themselves, blossoming careers, and apartments that were sun-drenched and airy, with wide original floorboards and canal views.

'You can make it happen!' the successful writer told Oprah's audience.

If only I could make something happen, I thought.

I'd heard that in the Netherlands it was possible to request an assisted suicide. One night, when I couldn't sleep, I called the crisis line to ask about it.

'What kind of help are you looking for?' asked the woman on the other end of the line.

'Assisted suicide,' I said. 'I'd like some advice on which pharmaceuticals to use. It wouldn't be a lot of work. I'd take the medicine myself, but it would be good to have someone to supervise me and make sure everything goes well.'

'Why do you want that?'

'Because I can't manage to get anything done on my own.'

'Why do you feel that way? Would you like to talk to a therapist about it?'

She asked too many questions. While I only had one question, which wasn't being answered.

My nose was itchy. I rubbed it without thinking, which made the straws fall out, which made me inhale some of the plaster. I picked at my nostril but couldn't get it out.

'She was so complicated,' said Thomas, 'and there was always something, but that was a good thing. Because if you have nothing going on, then you aren't truly living.'

I clapped my hands to get his attention, but at that very moment he pulled open one of his creaky kitchen cupboards.

'Now everything is grey again,' he said with his mouth full.

I crawled across the floor towards the kitchenette. On the way I hit my head on one of the table legs. The plaster cracked, and I scratched at it. Then I felt Thomas's warm hands on either side of my head. He stuck his fingers underneath the edges and gently removed the mask from my face. 'It wasn't fully attached,' he said.

That night, in bed, I stared at the ceiling. I don't exist, I thought. I'm something other people have made up. I tapped on the wall, and the rat briefly stopped gnawing.

Not Quite Traumatic

My grandma's kitchen had a little hatch that was used to pass plates full of delicious things from the kitchen to the living room. You could also throw a ball through it, but then you ran the risk of hitting the wooden figurines on the sideboard, and their thin legs were quite easy to break. They were valuable Indonesian wood carvings.

'Be careful, okay,' my mother would say if I even looked at them.

My grandma collected plastic butter containers. She had stacks of them in the kitchen cupboard. I understood from my parents that she did this because of the war. My father collected all kinds of electrical cables, which he also did because of the war. He kept boxes full of them in the garage. The war didn't worry my mother much. Every now and then, she'd secretly throw out some of his cables.

My grandma didn't say very much, but if my mother asked her about the war, she would respond as if telling a small child a scary story. She'd talk about everyone having to bow to 'the Japs' and how you were punished if you didn't do it properly, how some of the Japanese soldiers forced their prisoners to watch them torturing others, how she'd stand there with my father in the heat, her hands clamped on either side of his face to stop him from looking away, telling stories to distract him. When she shared these memories, my father would usually go into the kitchen to make some coffee. I listened, but would also keep an eye on the hatch. As soon as my father opened it, I would get up and take the bonbons from him. Then I'd squash the tops of the bonbons I liked most with my index finger, so no one else would choose them.

Red was my grandma's favourite colour. I wore her red earrings to her cremation. They were clip-ons, so it didn't matter that my ears weren't pierced. After a few hours, my earlobes really started to hurt, but I felt I should be able to cope with it for my grandma. She'd experienced far worse.

When my mother was cremated a few years later, my ears were pierced and I could wear dangly earrings. This time, the pain came from my mother's shoes: high-heeled sandals that were slightly too big for me, which meant that my feet slipped back and forth when I walked, and I developed huge blisters on both heels. I took them off during the speeches.

A few of the speakers recalled my mother's childhood, but I already knew all those stories. I looked over at my father. He was staring straight ahead, his stomach spilling over his tailored trousers. According to my grandma, hunger oedema had made his stomach swell when he was a child.

'What was the war like for you?' I asked him later that night. He shrugged. The only thing he could recall was a fence with a door in it.

My grandma said I should ask him more questions. She'd been dead for fifteen years when she said it. I had just graduated. I'd picked up my diploma that afternoon and was lying in bed with a packet of potato chips. Once I'd emptied the packet, I put it on top of my diploma, which was lying on my bedside table, and smoothed it out, just like my grandma had always done. She only ever bought chips when I was coming to visit, and she found it difficult to throw away the empty packets. I realised that I still knew very little about my father's wartime years. They had gone up in smoke along with my grandma and mother.

'Ask him more questions,' I heard my grandma say. 'It will do him good.' It was a thought that appeared suddenly in my head, but didn't seem to come from me.

I called my father, but he didn't pick up. I knew that he didn't believe the dead could speak.

'People will persuade themselves to believe anything,' he

often said. 'And sometimes they take it a bit far.'

He was set to retire in a week. At his farewell party, he wanted to sing Frank Sinatra's version of 'My Way'. I was going to accompany him on the piano, and had come over to his place a few days before the party so we could practise because Margaret, his girlfriend, wasn't very musically inclined.

Years ago, Margaret had moved from England to the Netherlands to do her PhD at a Dutch technical university. Now she taught there. My father's institution was next to Margaret's campus, separated only by a gym. It was there, by the rowing machines, that they first laid eyes on each other. Evening after evening, they rowed silently alongside each other until my father gathered all his courage and complimented her on her muscly calves.

Ever since then, he'd been acting strangely when I called.

'Pa.'

'Yes, darling!'

'Don't shout like that. Are you not alone?'

'No, Margaret is here. We're just about to buy some cheese and eggs at the farm stand. Is something wrong?'

She had a wide face and russet hair, light freckled skin, friendly pale blue eyes, and short legs with stocky calves from all the walking she did. According to my father, Margaret was extremely intelligent. She didn't yell at him, unless she had a migraine and he started doing his daily round with the dust buster. On weekends they took long walks together. My father had bought special walking shoes.

She didn't have any children herself, and did her best not to act like my mother when I came to stay with them. But she did speak up in defence of my father when I snapped at him for smacking his lips one night at dinner.

'He's not smacking his lips,' she said, 'he's using saliva to help him digest and swallow his food. Do you know what it would sound like if he didn't do that?' I was actually curious about that, but even though she was a physicist, she didn't know exactly how it would sound either. Margaret was a theorist and didn't care for the practical side of things.

At first, her soft voice, greying hair, and pale, almost transparent skin really bothered me. She had the kind of looks that my mother would have sarcastically referred to as 'all natural'. But the more I saw her, the more beautiful I began to find her. Except for her legs — they were too short.

Margaret helped me finish my thesis. I was studying comparative literature, not something she knew a great deal about, but that didn't matter. She reduced the uncontrollable variables down to a manageable number.

'There are some facts you're just better off ignoring,' she said.

She would only laugh if she found something funny, never for any other reason, and when I brought up something complicated, she usually kept quiet, even if it directly involved her, like my father's stacks. There were three stacks against the wall, between his recliner and the couch: newspapers from the past two months, brochures he still wanted to look through, and brochures he wanted to keep because they contained interesting discounts. In the kitchen, he didn't just have piles of tableware, he'd also stacked the washing machine, freezer and microwave on top of one another. Margaret had to stand on a stepping stool to reach the microwave. She had asked him to wash his duvet cover when it was dirty instead of turning it inside out to get one more use out of it, but she never laid out his clothes for him to wear the following morning, because she didn't care what he wore, even if he dressed himself in the same colour from head to toe. And she rarely went into the garage.

It was a Tuesday, three days before the retirement party. My father picked me up from the station in a green sweater, a slightly darker green pair of pants, dark green socks and grey-green shoes. His impending retirement didn't faze him, he said as we drove home, but he wasn't exactly looking forward to it either. He didn't have a plan for how he was going to fill his days, and that did concern him a little.

'Maybe you could clean out the garage,' I said, as we turned into our street.

'But it's already quite organised.' My father had even stacked up all the boxes full of cables.

Margaret was standing in the kitchen over a large pot of vegetable soup.

'Hi dear,' she said. 'We'll eat in around ten minutes.' Large chunks of carrot and leek were floating around in the bouillon. She always made soup without meatballs. My father thought everything was delicious, as long as there was enough of it. He put on a CD while she set the table. When he passed by and slapped her playfully on the bum, she responded with a polite little British squeal. Was she aware that the seams of her underwear were visible through her jeans, I wondered. Some people never look at their backside in the mirror.

'Are you sure you want to sing that Frank Sinatra song?' I asked during dinner.

'Yes,' said my father. 'It'll be funny.'

Margaret inspected her cuticles.

Lots of his friends were coming to the party, in addition to his colleagues and some of his patients. Betsy would probably also be there. She had been his patient for more than twenty years. I'd met her a few times while visiting my father at the institution. Sometimes she behaved quite normally, but if you disagreed with her, she'd start ranting and hiss, 'Get a disease!' as if it were a curse. My father advised me to say, 'Gosh, is that what you really think, Betsy?' if she ever shared her opinion on something, because that's how he always responded. She often giggled when he was around. She said that he put good thoughts in her head.

When I was a child, I thought that Betsy had made my mother sick the day she came to pick me up from the institution. It was during the school holidays, and my mother had an audition, so she'd brought me to my father, who had given me a pile of comics and left me at the on-site café. The woman behind the counter was supposed keep an eye on me, and he would come back later to check on things, he said, between patients. Betsy was sitting at the counter, dipping her fingers into a packet of peanuts and watching the television hanging from the corner of the ceiling. It was showing a documentary about insects. Occasionally, Betsy would yell something at the screen. In my comic book, a large man with two plaits was ramming the heads of two thin men wearing dresses against each other. I imagined punching Betsy so hard she'd fall off her chair, then I'd kick her until she crawled out of the café screaming. Maybe then my father would come out of his office.

When the insect documentary ended, Betsy slid off her barstool and walked towards me. I bent quickly over my comic book, but her pink legs lingered at my table. The television was playing the theme song of a quiz show. Betsy sat down next to me. The contestants had to make the longest words they could from a selection of letters. But first they took turns asking for vowels and consonants.

'Another vowel,' said Betsy, but the contestant asked for a consonant. 'Vowel,' she shrieked.

'Vowel,' said another one of the participants, an older man in a suit. According to Betsy, she had a telepathic connection with him. We started playing along with the contestants, making words from the available letters.

'Hat,' said Betsy.

'Hatter,' I said.

'Yeah,' said Betsy. 'I just said that.'

The contestant in the suit said 'cupola'. I didn't think

that was an actual word, but Betsy said it was. She was just getting wound up when my mother walked in.

'Has your father come to check on you?' she asked me. He hadn't. My mother sighed.

'I did see him this morning,' said Betsy, 'in the hallway.' She straightened her back and looked at my mother. 'Here you are then, with your red lipstick.'

'Yes,' said my mother, 'here I am.' She started telling me about the errands we had to run.

'Can you shut your trap for a moment?' Betsy snapped. 'I can't hear what they're saying.' She pointed at the TV.

'Then go and sit a bit closer to it,' said my mother.

That was the last straw for Betsy. She turned red and started screaming at my mother, telling her to get a disease and go to hell, before turning her attention back to the television. Afterwards I was fairly certain I'd also heard her whisper 'cancer' several times.

A year later, shortly after my eleventh birthday, my mother got sick. It was only after her operation and first round of chemo, when my father dropped one of my mother's antique vases and yelled, 'Oh, bloody hell,' that I thought about Betsy and how she sometimes looked possessed, like Carrie, from the Stephen King novel, only quite a bit older. I wondered how to go about breaking a curse. My mother was attempting to do it by telling herself in the mirror that she wasn't going to die and imagining tiny soldiers who fought off the cancer cells at night. But none of it would be necessary if I hadn't spoken to Betsy that day. I hoped to lift the curse by becoming a better person, walking the dog more often, eating less, and, most importantly, not thinking any bad thoughts. At first it seemed to help just enough, because my mother remained sick but didn't die. Then it didn't help at all. Betsy won. And for a while afterwards I had lots of bad thoughts.

In her final days, my grandma would only talk about her eldest son's fingernails, which the Japs had put in an envelope for her. To be honest, I'm no longer sure it was an envelope, and my father wasn't sure either. He could only remember his brother from the photos on the dresser, he said. We'd just practised his retirement song and were sitting on the couch.

'Wait a minute.' He walked into the kitchen and came back with a bowl of peanuts and two tumblers, half filled with jenever. He'd once read somewhere that a handful of peanuts a day could keep dementia at bay.

'Do you still eat those?' I asked.

'Of course,' he said. 'It can't do any harm. Your grandma started showing signs of it in her sixties.'

Whenever you asked my grandma how it was going, she'd always respond with: 'Oh, it's going.' But then, she couldn't remember that she'd taken the bus down to the tulip fields that afternoon, and that I'd been sitting next to her. She was amazed by the white stripes on the streets and how they'd managed to make them so perfectly straight and that everyone was so good at staying between the lines. My father had installed her telephone, her television and her alarm clock. Afterwards she'd pulled out all their electrical cables, rolled them up, and secured them with tape. On the night she died, he was sitting beside her bed. He'd stroked her face to close her eyes, but she'd opened them, so he had to do it again.

'What is that you're afraid of forgetting?' I asked my father.

'I'm not afraid,' he said, 'but I wouldn't like to forget that you had been to visit me, for example, or that I'd taken a lovely walk with Margaret. Or who Margaret is, I wouldn't like to forget that either.'

'Or who Mama was.'

'I won't forget that. You don't forget the distant past.'

'You do,' I said.

He laughed.

What he could remember from his childhood were the flying fish they saw in the Red Sea on their way from Singapore to the Netherlands, and the British soldiers who'd given them a lift in their jeep. They'd driven extra fast, just for my father. He'd felt the wind in his hair, and everyone had laughed.

'But all of that happened after the war,' I said.

'Yes,' he said. 'Are you finished with that?' He wanted to take my glass, which was still a quarter full, back to the kitchen.

'Not yet,' I said.

He leant back and looked straight ahead.

'Okay then,' he said, and started telling me about a therapy group he'd attended when he was still training to be a psychiatrist. During one of the group sessions, he'd experienced something that came close to a traumatic memory. The memory that wasn't entirely traumatic had made him cry, he said, but not miserably. It was an image of water, and he could see a sphere coming up from the deep, but the image evaporated before it could reach the surface.

'The sphere stayed beneath the surface,' he said, 'and I still don't know if I'm supposed to feel bad about that or not.'

'And what would have happened if the sphere had made it to the surface?' I asked.

'Maybe it would have exploded,' said my father. 'I'm not sure.' He picked up my glass and took it into the kitchen.

I followed him.

'Why are you so uninterested in what happened during the war?' I asked. My glass was on the kitchen counter. I finished the jenever and put it back.

'It's not that,' he said. 'When you were little, your grandma offered to take me back to Indonesia, but I chose to go to France with you and your mother instead. I would like to see Indonesia, for sure, but I'd also quite like to see Australia or Peru.' He used a cloth to wipe the fingerprints off the fridge. 'I want the past to be colourless.'

○

My father wore various shades of blue to his retirement party. Margaret was in a purple blouse and a nice pair of black pants, but no high heels. She really should have worn heels. From my seat at the grand piano, I watched her speaking with one of my father's colleagues. Betsy was standing in line for the buffet with her plate in hand, scowling as she looked at the salads and savoury tarts. She was shorter than I remembered her, but her skin was still as pink as ever. There was a brightly coloured headband in her frizzy grey hair.

I started to play and my father began to sing. He walked back and forth across the stage with his microphone, as if he were an accomplished performer. Everyone was smiling at him, but my father took it very seriously. He did a good job of building up to the chorus, and refrained from immediately going all out, just as we'd rehearsed.

When he got to the first hook, the part about biting off 'more than I could chew', his voice rose. Thankfully, he could sing.

'Ahhhhhh,' I sang along. The crescendo was approaching and he bent slightly, put the microphone just below his face and gave it his all. When he got to the part about saying the things he truly feels and not the words of one who kneels, he looked up at the sky.

Then he stood up and slicked back his hair, flattening it so he looked like a mechanic. Suddenly, I got a little flustered. What if his voice skipped over the last part.

But he sang the final line flawlessly.

Everyone clapped, a few people cheered, Margaret smiled widely, Betsy stared, my father kept knocking the microphone against the clamp on the side of the stand, I walked over to him, the microphone slid into the clamp, my father slicked his hair back again, I grabbed his hand and together, we gave a deep bow.

Don't Die

I was sitting in the glass ticket booth at the museum. There was a long queue of tourists at the door, waiting to come in so they could look at photos of overcrowded trains and piled-up skeletons. When the door opened, the queue slowly began to move.

Most of the museum's visitors put their money silently in the designated tray, and then they would stare at their money and wait. Look at me, I thought. I'd look into their empty eyes through the glass window and wait for the panic to set in. It always did. Some people pushed their money against the window, repeatedly stubbing their fingers. Others turned around, seeking support from the people standing behind them. After a while, they would all look at me, confused. And that was the moment I'd choose to press the button on my microphone.

'Good morning,' I'd say. 'Can I help you?'

It was a small museum, which meant that sometimes the doors had to close to stop it from becoming overfull. When this happened, I would stick a sign to my window and grab a book from my bag. Today, it was a book of short stories by Lydia Davis. I opened the book to a random page and started reading. The story was called 'A Double Negative'. It was about a woman who, at a certain point in her life, realises that it's not so much that she wants to have a child as that she doesn't want not to have a child, or not to have had one. It was a very short story. I read it for a second time. 'Don't have children until you've accomplished something in life,' my mother often said. When I was ten, I promised myself I'd wait until I was twenty-six to have children. Meanwhile, I'd turned thirty-three. A tourist tapped on the window.

'How much longer?' she asked.

When I was twenty-six, I dated a man who was thirty-eight. Together, we looked down on women his age who were obsessed with having kids. They were an inferior kind.

'It's almost as if they suddenly lose the capacity to use their brains,' he said, while stroking my tight bum. His ex-girlfriend was also that kind of woman. And I was certain I wouldn't become one of them.

Around the age of thirty-three, I became that kind of woman, but I decided to be open and honest about it. Some women my age suppressed the urge to become a mother and tried desperately to overcompensate by attempting to impress men with their intelligence and desire for freedom. But I noticed that it really was possible to long for a child and use my intellect at the same time.

'You always need to define everything,' said the men I tended to fall in love with. 'These things just have to develop naturally.' One of them didn't have a phone. Another one never answered his phone. And naturally, they ended up vanishing from my life. Whenever I found myself single again, I would withdraw and watch TV.

'You have to stay visible,' said a former television presenter who had agreed to be locked in a house with nine other famous Dutch people where they would be filmed twenty-four hours a day. I should also remember to do that, I thought, stay visible. The presenter had gathered all her housemates for a meeting. She said that after showering, she always pulled her hair out of the drain, and she asked the others to do the same.

I'd just come out of a long period of TV-watching when I met Philip. After our second night together, he left his contact lens solution in my bathroom. 'This way I won't have to keep bringing it over,' he said.

He called me his girlfriend, even when his friends were around. We went to parties and barbeques together. Once we were home, he'd often complain about someone saying something that had rubbed him the wrong way. People were constantly saying things that rubbed him the wrong way. We discussed his work, his mother's coldness and his problematic feet. He had a condition that made his feet sweat excessively. I wasn't supportive enough, he said.

He gave me the key to his house and soon after that stopped looking up from his computer screen when I let myself in. Sometimes he'd say he wasn't sure if he still loved me.

Some of his friends joined us for a holiday on an island in the Mediterranean Sea. They were a couple with a six-year-old son who ran naked through the garden of our rental house every morning while waving a *Star Wars* lightsaber. I taught him how to cheat at cards and jumped on beds with him until I had to throw up all the Baileys I drank that day. He slept with his parents in the room next to ours, so Philip and I had to whisper when we argued at night. After a week of this, we broke up in a series of whispers.

Two days later it was my birthday. Philip and I sat on the beach under a parasol, holding cocktails. All the tension had exhausted us but we were also quite relieved. I said I was afraid of not living and just spending my life standing on the sidelines. 'Recently I've realised that it's not so much that I want to have a child,' I said, 'it's more that I don't want not to have a child, or not to have had one.' He said he'd once seen me snap at his friend's kid and that made him wonder if I had the capacity to be a good mother.

After that holiday, I had a moustache. When I googled

it, I read that pregnant women can develop pigmentation on their upper lip. But you can also develop a moustache from stress.

Two years later, I was riding my bike against oncoming traffic when I almost ran into someone.

'Bitch!' cried the woman.

'There's no need to swear,' I said.

'No,' she said, 'but I have a child on the back of my bike.' Behind her was a little blonde girl sitting on a plastic throne.

People who have children think they can get away with anything, I thought on my way to the café. It had started raining. I pictured my mother's jacket in front of me and the way it flapped in my face whenever I sat behind her on her bike. I'd never really thought about it, though I usually did my best to remember details like that. Worst of all, I'd forgotten the sound of her voice.

The café was crowded. I spotted Thomas standing at the back of the room. We used to spend a lot of time watching TV together when he was still living around the corner from me, but he'd gotten into a serious relationship with a jealous woman, and we had lost touch.

I threaded my way through all the sweaty smells and damp jackets until I was standing before him. Thomas was surprised to see me. He and the jealous woman had two daughters and work was going well, he said. He was on the verge of breaking through internationally.

'Two daughters,' I said. 'How nice.'

He asked if I still worked at the museum — he'd seen me sitting there a few years ago.

'I was in a rush, otherwise I would have stopped,' he said.

I remembered seeing him ride past on a bike with children's seats on the back of it and acting as if I suddenly had to pick up something from the floor.

'No, I write for a newspaper now,' I said. 'Interviews.' He nodded. I nodded too. Both of us looked down at our beers. Then I told him that I also wanted to have a child, but none of my relationships had lasted long enough to start trying. 'And I'll be thirty-six soon.' My eyes started to burn.

'Oh, God,' he said, 'does everything still look grey to you?'

At home I watched a talk show in which a doctor spoke about women who didn't have any children, despite wanting them.

'It's like having a chronic illness,' he said. 'Involuntary childlessness has a significant effect on you. It stays with you for the rest of your life.'

I called a friend who was quite a bit older than me and didn't have any children. 'It's too late for me,' she said, 'but you could still have a child if you want to. You'll really need to start focusing on it, though.' She had ADHD, which meant that it wasn't easy for her to focus. Whenever I told her anything, I had to speak very quickly, so I could finish before her thoughts strayed.

○

The first thing I noticed about Arthur was his furrowed brow and his wild hair.

'I'm Arthur,' he said. His voice was a little higher than I'd expected. The furrowed brow disappeared when he smiled.

He'd designed a violent video game that had gone viral around the world. I interviewed him for the newspaper. The interview should focus on death, my editor told me, and what it's like to spend every day thinking up new ways to destroy people.

'I enjoy it,' said Arthur. 'The trick is to make it as realistic as possible.' As a child, he'd been so frightened of monsters that he'd barely been able to sleep at night. To cure himself, he'd started watching horror films. Now he could watch the most horrific scenes without any fear. He was mostly interested in learning how the scenes were produced. When I asked if he was religious, he made a face. 'I'm not afraid of death,' he said. 'So, I don't have any need for religion.' Funeral rituals didn't interest him either. They could hang him upside down and naked from a church tower when he died, if that's what they wanted to do. I told him that I also wasn't afraid, but I found it a shame. People who feared death were often very productive. They wanted to leave something behind. I spent most of my time lying on the couch.

'It's almost like being dead,' I said.

Arthur said he was still a very productive person. This reassured me a little.

He emailed to tell me there was a spelling mistake in the third paragraph but otherwise found it one of the best interviews he'd read in the past ten years. I wondered which interviews he'd found better eleven years ago. After that, we kept on emailing each other. One morning, three weeks after the interview, I went outside and found him at my door. He was just about to slide an envelope into my letter box.

'I'm not stalking you, okay,' he said. Embarrassed, he handed me the envelope. We had been emailing about an Italian mafia series that he really liked. He'd copied every season of the show onto a DVD for me. That day, we watched the first few episodes while sitting very close to each other on my large couch.

Arthur had an enormous flat-screen television, and it was on that screen that I played his video game for the first time.

'Why isn't my puppet moving anymore?' I asked. 'I don't want to see all the scenes with explanations.' Impatient, I pressed all the buttons until my puppet started moving again.

'They aren't puppets,' said Arthur, 'they're characters, and there's a plot.' The game was about a civilisation that had long ago been exiled to another planet filled with poisonous gas, and they had developed noses like anteaters and scaly skin. They had an ugly but charismatic leader who encouraged his followers to take back their terrestrial paradise by force.

'Beautiful, isn't it,' said Arthur as I shot half of someone's head off. The victim, a woman, sank slowly to her knees and lay the other half of her head at my feet, exposing the side I had gutted.

'He's such a sweet boy,' said Arthur's mother. We were sitting at an Italian restaurant. Arthur had just walked outside to help his father with the parking meter. His father had the same wild hair as Arthur, only a little thinner. His mother had his eyes, without the furrowed brow. 'He's very caring,' she said. I nodded and thought of the little Japanese porcelain bowl he used to serve chocolates after a meal. He always made sure there were a few white chocolates in the bowl, because I really liked them. And the coffee, I thought, I shouldn't forget to mention the coffee. There was an enormous espresso machine in his tiny kitchen.

'He's very good at making coffee,' I said, and looked at his sister, who was sitting opposite me, staring at something on her phone. Then I studied my serviette.

'I googled you,' said his mother. 'Your interviews are nicely written.' She leant towards me. 'Arthur says that he could really see it working out with you.' Her lack of shame comforted me. His sister was done with her phone.

'Don't listen to my mother,' she said. 'She's crazy.'

Arthur's father's eyebrows were so long that they almost covered his eyes. During dinner he said he'd studied Hotel Management and worked at five-star hotels until he retired. He'd started as a waiter and ended up a manager. It was a shame, he said, that his son had never worked in hospitality.

'He has a flair for it,' said Arthur's father, raising his eyebrows. He's scared, I thought, when I saw his eyes. I wondered if he had managed hotels with those brows or if he'd let them grow after retiring.

'It was only when I turned twenty-six,' said Arthur's mother 'and met people who'd chosen not to have children that I realised it was also an option. But by that time, I already had two of them.' We were sitting in the garden of their farmhouse, and Arthur was helping his father repair the pond pump. At first, she'd found it very hard, she said, because Arthur's father was always at the hotel. And apart from that she'd struggled with herself. Arthur had mentioned that his mother had often sat in the closet, crying amongst her homemade dresses and colourful scarves.

Arthur and his father came to sit with us. His father was sweating. Drops of sweat slid down his forehead into his eyebrows.

'The pump is fixed,' he said, 'but the roof still needs to be repaired and so does the gate for the donkeys. I'm not sure how I'm supposed to find the time to do all of that.' His voice kept increasing in volume and pitch.

'Maybe you should get rid of the donkeys,' said Arthur.

'Are you crazy,' said his father. 'Onno and Jack aren't going anywhere.' He stood up and went inside.

'I think he might be close to another burnout,' said Arthur's mother.

On the way to the cinema, for a zombie game release party, Arthur asked if I wanted children.

'Yes,' I said. 'Do you?' We were walking our bikes across a square. A souped-up moped sped past us. Arthur shouted something at the driver, and the driver stuck his middle finger in the air. I stared at my handlebars.

'I don't,' said Arthur. 'Not anymore.' We looked for a place for our bikes in front of the cinema. 'Come,' said Arthur, 'put your bike over here, and I'll put mine in front of it.' He pointed at a vacant piece of wall. I felt like I wanted to throw up. When I eventually looked up from my bike, I saw two zombies walking into the cinema. He used to want them, Arthur explained, but now he thought he was too old. Aside from that, he knew that children took over your life. All the fathers he knew looked completely worn out. The only thing I can remember from the rest of that evening is the zombies wandering the halls of the theatre, their shabby Nikes dragging across the thick carpet.

Arthur cleared out a shelf in his closet and bought a white waffle-weave dressing gown for me.

'Don't die,' he said whenever I went outside. We talked about having children in bed at night, when it was dark, and we couldn't see each other. He sounded depressed, and I'd usually cry. Once, he cried too, while telling me about his father, his mother, his ex-girlfriend and all the other people he'd helped and how he'd done his best to make their lives easier. 'I can't worry about one more person,' he said. Arthur had lived with his ex-girlfriend for ten years. When he spoke about her, he used short sentences. She'd had a difficult childhood. At her core, she was a good person. They hadn't ended up having a child.

I decided to drop the subject and hoped that eventually I'd know what to do. In the meantime, I took driving lessons.

Rudy of Rudy's Driving School was around fifty and lived in a flat in Diemen. His mother lived a few streets away from him. She brought him soup when he was sick. On weekends, Rudy would put on his leather pants and head out to the gay bars. He said he could never be in a relationship with me because I said, 'oh, yeah,' far too much for his liking. Whenever Rudy needed to pee, he'd tell me to stop so he could piss against a hedge or a wall. Some mornings, I asked him to pick me up at Arthur's place, and then he'd ask me if I'd gotten laid.

My first driving lessons were a blur. 'Brake, brake, brake,' Rudy kept saying. At his insistence, I used a plate and a cucumber to practise steering and changing gears while sitting on the couch. After a few months, we drove onto the highway.

'Knowledge is power, also when you're merging,' said Rudy. Whenever we passed a beautiful man, he'd say: 'Look at that sexy thing.'

'Oh, come on,' I'd say, and then he'd say: 'I'm allowed to look!'

According to him, my biggest challenge while driving was the fact that I didn't look properly.

'What is this!' he'd cry, as I made the same mistakes

over and over again. I tried to convince him that there was nothing he could do, that he was merely an artist working with inferior tools.

Arthur had to go to Morocco to photograph locations for his team to use as model landscapes for a new game they were developing. I went with him as his assistant and interpreter. Our guide drove us around from sunrise to sunset. Arthur bent, squatted, crawled and climbed in order to capture every single detail of each location. I followed him around carrying his camera bag. Occasionally, I'd rest on a bench. Our guide would talk to people passing by or stare into space. He ate dinner with us every night. If I asked him a question, he'd either ignore me or mumble something incomprehensible in French.

At the Hyatt hotel in Casablanca, Arthur and I were drinking wine in the lobby, enjoying our first moment alone together. The waiter brought our glasses. When he asked if I wanted some peanuts or olives, I couldn't choose and my face turned red. Arthur said he'd never seen me so timid. He noticed I'd been subdued all week. I said it was probably because of our guide and because of all the short people in Morocco. Short people made me uncomfortable.

'Relax,' he said, looking around uneasily. He probably wanted to go to bed.

In bed we got into an argument about a hotel I'd wanted to book a few days prior, when we had driven north. The hotel was an old palace in the medina of Fez that had been renovated by a Danish couple. My newspaper had published an article on it in the culture section. Our guide said he didn't know it. But later, when we stopped at a roadside restaurant so I could go to the toilet, he managed to convince Arthur that we could find a better place to stay. His friends also had a hotel in Fez.

'Set it up,' Arthur had told him, and when I returned from the toilet it was already organised.

'I was tired,' Arthur said now. 'I had a lot on my mind. You could have cancelled his hotel.' I said that I didn't want to cause any trouble, that I'd done my best to blend into the background for the entire trip, so I wouldn't stress him out, and that I was supposed to be the one who arranged our hotels, but the guide refused to accept anything I tried to initiate, to which Arthur yelled that I shouldn't give a shit what the guide thought, that he'd actually welcome more initiative from my side, like noticing that he needed a phone card, for example, and I shouted that I didn't like his tone. We continued on like this until Arthur turned to me and said: 'You don't have to blend into the background for me, I'd much rather have you here. You're so great when you're right here with me.'

Once he was asleep, I slipped into the bathroom, where I took a bath and finally relaxed. The next day I bought three telephone cards for the price of two. Eight hundred minutes of call time in total.

When we returned from Morocco, I had infected

earlobes. Rudy thought they looked disgusting. The weather was gorgeous, and we were driving to Zandvoort beach. When we reached the boulevard, we got out of the car and looked at the sea for a moment.

'Shall we get going?' Rudy asked.

On the way home I ran over a partridge.

'You couldn't help it,' said Rudy. 'It was either him or us.'

At home, Arthur was making parmigiana di melanzane. I looked for a space to put my contact lens holder between all the aubergines and tomatoes on the kitchen counter. Driving always hurt my eyes. Arthur began slicing an aubergine, and I told him about the partridge. After that, Arthur told me about a dying dog he'd seen in Thailand long ago. The dog had lain next to a pile of garbage near the beach for days. Eventually, Arthur had taken a piece of wood and hit the dog hard on its head.

'I had to,' he said. 'No one was doing anything to help it.'

It occurred to me then that he would make a good father.

Arthur's parents were on holiday, and we were looking after their donkeys. They let Arthur rub their noses and ate apples from his hand. When I tried to feed them, they'd turn their rumps to me. Next to the farm was a small forest, where miniature ponies galloped in the evening light. At night, I listened to the wind in the trees and thought about people with kids who say 'join the club' to freshly minted parents, and people with kids who say having children really isn't that great. They were often the same people who, after their first child, decided to have two more. And these people also believe that you don't just have children, they are given to you.

One rainy afternoon, we were sitting next to each other on the couch in the farmhouse with our laptops on our laps. I was reading a website about teeth whitening, and Arthur was searching for a salad spinner on Facebook marketplace when he suddenly stopped scrolling and looked sideways.

'I want to do it,' he said. 'Have a child. Shall we just go for it?'

I looked at him.

'Really?'

He nodded. 'But if it doesn't work out, I hope you can still be happy with just me.'

I could. Suddenly, I was very sure of it.

My parking wasn't perfect, and I attempted to drive off in third gear, but I managed to pass my driving test. The examiner's name was Sjoerd. While we were driving, he told me he had four kids. After the fourth was born, he'd had the snip.

'Congratulations,' said Rudy when I was done. 'You only just squeaked through.' When we turned into our street, Arthur rode up on his bike. I asked Rudy if he was relieved that I hadn't brought down his average pass rate.

'A little bit, yeah,' he said, 'but now you're leaving a gap in my income.' He watched with interest as Arthur locked his bike.

I said that I knew other people like me and would recommend they all take lessons with him.

'That would be great,' he said, then fished a business card out of his pocket.

Once we were inside, Arthur brought out a bottle of champagne and two party hats. When the bottle was empty, he took off his party hat.

'Come on,' he said, 'otherwise there won't be any baby.'

Arthur's Little Cough

When I was fifteen, I took volleyball lessons for a few months and before every match we'd shout: 'Spirit hey, spirit hey, spirit active, hey, hey, hey.' I thought about this when I woke up. The baby was kicking me, and I lay my hand on my belly. It wasn't so long ago that I thought pregnant women who always had a hand on their belly were stupid. Everything about pregnant women seemed stupid to me.

'You're very hard on your pregnancy,' my friend with ADHD told me. 'It's almost as if you're not enjoying it.' This surprised me. Then I remembered what she'd said to me when I first met Arthur: 'It's almost as if you don't dare to laugh.'

The day before, we'd had our twenty-week ultrasound. From the beginning of the pregnancy, I'd imagined our daughter to be a girl with straight brown hair and a long fringe. I could picture her standing in the schoolyard, her head slightly bowed and her fingers intertwined, just as I'd once been photographed. The photo was taken on my first day of school, and you can see my mother in the background, wearing a yellow summer dress. She is looking sideways at one of the other mothers and seems distracted. What if I have a child and it dies, I thought. Imagine if my daughter drowned in a stream while I was looking the other way. You also have to focus if you want to prevent things from happening.

'It's a boy,' the sonographer had said.

He was born on a Saturday morning. And he got stuck. I kept screaming and thinking about the bedroom window, which was open. At exactly eleven o'clock, the doorbell rang and he fell out of me. We never found out who was at the door that morning.

For a second, I thought there was a calf lying on our wooden floor. The baby was enormous and vaguely blue. The midwife bent over him.

'Can I hold him?' I asked.

She looked up. 'No,' she said. Then she cut his umbilical cord and walked away with the baby.

'Follow them,' I said to Arthur.

The maternity nurse had just put my placenta into a plastic bag when we heard the baby crying. But only briefly before it went quiet. I was allowed to walk carefully into the living room, where I found the baby was lying on the table. The midwife was holding a telephone to her ear. She was wearing plastic gloves that were covered in poo. Her other hand was holding an oxygen mask on the baby's face. In the meantime, the baby had turned a deep pink. The maternity nurse took me over to the couch. I was just lying down on it when five paramedics came in and stood between me and the baby. One of them did something with a tube, then put the baby on a tiny stretcher. Arthur was allowed to go with him. I was going to follow in the second ambulance.

'Can you walk?' asked my paramedic. 'Otherwise, we'll use the winch to lift you out.'

I walked slowly down three flights of stairs wearing a kaftan I'd bought in Morocco. The trim was the same fluorescent yellow as the stripes on my paramedic's uniform.

We couldn't find the right department at the hospital. The paramedic rolled me through various hallways, and we rode the elevator twice before we found the baby again. There were all kinds of tubes attached to him and patches on his chest. The nurse put him in my arms, and for a moment, it felt like I woke up.

I shared a room with a woman who kept snorting when she cried. Her baby was also in an incubator. He had also gotten stuck. Every day she would call multiple people to tell them how traumatic the birth had been for her, and how the midwife hadn't listened when she had told her that she was a ballerina, and everyone knew about ballerinas and their pelvic floor muscles: they were far too strong to let a baby through. At night, she smacked her lips in her sleep. There were curtains around our beds, which the nurse would open every morning because she thought we needed light. But I didn't need any light. Several times a day, while walking over to the NICU, I'd pass a sign that gave directions to the madhouse. It felt as if years had passed since I had been there, but in truth it had only been six weeks.

All the counters and walls in the madhouse were covered in a layer of wood veneer, and in my new woollen jacket it felt like I was walking into a ski resort. Shortly after checking in at the anxiety desk, I was picked up by a man in a white coat. He was a research-psychologist-in-training, he said. 'I'm a patient-to-be,' I said. He looked at my enormous belly and laughed nervously. Then we walked in silence through a large corridor. I had difficulty keeping up with him. He was wearing sneakers, the ugly leather kind. Arthur always called that kind of men's dress sneakers 'The Shoe'. I thought about Arthur and how, in the evenings, he would sit next to me on the couch, trying to chew his biscuit as quietly as possible.

'This treatment is still in the research phase,' said the psychologist-in-training once we were seated in his office. 'But first, we need to decide if you're eligible to participate in the study.' He put a list of multiple-choice questions in front of me. 'Question one,' he said. 'How many times a day do you find yourself bothered by difficult sounds?'

'Answer b,' I said.

The psychologist-in-training nodded. 'Question two. Which five sounds do you find the most difficult?'

'Lip-smacking,' I said. 'Then swallowing, coughing, snorting or sniffing and nail-biting.' These were all on his list. He put a tick next to them.

Once we'd gone through the list of questions, I was told to wait in the corridor for the psychiatrist. I was startled when he came out of his office. He looked like a film star.

'I'm John,' he said. The completed questionnaire was lying on his desk. 'Do you sleep well?' he asked. His eyes were terribly blue.

'Not so well but that's because of my pregnancy. I have restless legs.' I quickly hid my feet under the chair. My ankles were thick and swollen.

'And before the pregnancy?'

'I also slept badly then, but that was because I was on my own for so long, and later, when I wasn't alone anymore, it was because the tempo of my boyfriend's breathing is different from my own.'

He wrote something in the margin of the questionnaire. We spoke a while longer about the sounds I found difficult, and what I thought about when I couldn't sleep. Then John said: 'I think you worry excessively. Which is why you'd be a good candidate for the treatment we're offering.'

I felt my face getting warm. 'Oh, okay,' I said. 'That's good to know.'

The baby's name was Bob. After three days, he was able to leave the incubator, and we all went home. Our bedroom felt like a crime scene scrubbed clean. I put Bob on the neatly made bed.

'You should try to get some sleep,' said Arthur. 'The maternity nurse will be here soon.'

Bob yawned and groaned and smacked his lips, and I kissed him and thought about how my mother always used to plant big smackers on my ears.

According to the maternity nurse, Bob was the biggest baby she'd ever seen, apart from Alain Clark's baby.

Arthur coughed.

'I'd prefer it if you just cleared your throat loudly once instead of continuing to do all those little coughs.'

'But I don't need to clear my throat loudly,' said Arthur. 'I need to do the little coughs.'

He also said that we had run out of coffee and was grabbing his jacket when the phone rang. It was someone who worked at the madhouse.

'You can join the December group,' she said. 'We start in two weeks. I'll email you the roster.'

It was group therapy. I hadn't been expecting that.

That night I googled Alain Clark. After that, I googled the behavioural therapists listed on the roster. All of them had Facebook accounts. One of them was pictured sitting sweaty-faced over a plate of Vietnamese spring rolls. Another therapist was standing on a mountain in a pair of shorts, waving a little white flag at me.

'If our breathing cycles get too out of sync, then I sleep badly,' I told the therapist. We were sitting at a large table in a small room at the madhouse: Brian, Kees, Jona, Marleen and me. The therapist was standing beside a whiteboard and was breathing very loudly through her nose. She'd asked everyone to tell the group something about themselves.

Brian's girlfriend made crackling sounds when she ate. They hadn't had sex in a while. He looked at me sideways. 'How do you sit so incredibly still,' he said.

Jona said that lip-smacking, sniffly noses, clicking pens, the click-clack of high heels on a hard floor, crinkling packets and men who breathed loudly all made her aggressive. Which is why she spent most of her time at home with her cat.

As a child, Marleen had already found it strange that when people got into relationships they'd start sleeping in the same bed. And that was it. You'd just sleep in the same bed for the rest of your life.

'Do you find it difficult to lie next to your boyfriend in bed?' asked the therapist.

'I make it work,' said Marleen, 'but he can't cuddle up to me, because it makes me crazy.'

Brian started nodding wildly beside me.

'I would like it if I could learn not to panic when my

girlfriend's mouth comes close to my ear.' He pointed at a photo in a brochure lying on the table. A young woman was leaning over a man's shoulder while laughing. 'We can't do that,' he said.

It was quiet for a moment. Then the therapist asked if he expected he'd ever be able to do it.

'Yes, I hope so,' he said, 'otherwise I wouldn't be sitting here.'

'Great,' said the therapist. She wanted to wrap things up.

Outside the madhouse, I bought an apple turnover from a woman wearing a Santa hat.

Of all the difficult sounds, unnecessary sounds were the most difficult. Chewing with your mouth open was unnecessary. Taking enormous bites was unnecessary, as was chewing too quickly, or sighing softly after swallowing. My father took enormous bites of everything and would shove all of his food into one cheek then start talking. If I ever commented on it when I was younger, he'd say that he didn't have to be so polite in front of his own wife and daughter. I felt that he did. It made no sense to show your most disgusting side to the people you loved most. My mother agreed. She held it together until she couldn't anymore.

Arthur took normal-sized bites, chewed with his mouth closed, and usually only spoke once he'd swallowed everything. But he did occasionally get things stuck between his teeth and would then put his tongue against it and suck.

Which is why we listened to music while we ate.

Before meeting him, I'd briefly dated a man who bit his nails. He'd throw the nails on the ground or the garbage bin or the empty cola can that he kept in his car specifically for that purpose. I asked him if he wouldn't mind closing the door to the toilet after he went and putting the butter back in the fridge when he was finished with it, but what I actually wanted to ask was if he could stop sniffing, take smaller bites of his sandwiches, and whether he would ever stop biting his nails. When I finally brought up his nails, he shouted that I typed too loudly and he'd been unable to concentrate the whole morning because of it.

A few years later, I ran into him in the bread section at the supermarket. He told me that he was in a happy relationship with a woman. I told him about Arthur and said that I was also happy. And we stood opposite each other for a moment, both of us happy. When I got to the check-out, he was also there, paying for his shopping. I quickly chose a different line. While I packed up my shopping, he walked past me on his way out and acted as if he didn't notice me.

Arthur and I lived in a small studio apartment. He could see me wherever I went, except the toilet, or if I went to stand behind the room divider, which was where we'd put Bob's bed. Whenever Arthur changed his nappy or put him to bed, I could hear them gurgling. He was teaching Bob how to make zombie noises.

'Babies don't find it scary,' he said. At six years old, he had discovered zombies while watching the film *Night of the Living Dead*. He'd hidden himself underneath the blankets for nights on end, finding he could breathe in the gap between the wall and his bed. After that, he'd gone on to see almost every zombie film ever made.

'If you spend enough time exposing yourself to the things you cannot stand, eventually you'll become immune to them.'

'Not me,' I said. 'I would go crazy.'

In the evenings, Arthur and I would sit on the couch with our laptops. He often looked at the kind of websites where people upload funny pictures. To see those pictures, you'd first have to scroll through pictures of things that weren't as funny: photos of dead bodies or bald men sticking their heads into vaginas. According to Arthur, that was a porn genre. He wasn't a fan of it, but he had to go through those photos to get to the funny ones. If he found a picture particularly funny, he would have a laughing fit, and I would watch him until it was over. Sometimes I'd look at the picture too, but I preferred to look at him.

Before we went to sleep, we'd ask each other who-do-you-like-more questions. Who do you like more: Vivienne Westwood or Frida Kahlo, fries or shawarma, you or me? He asked me George Bush or Ted Bundy, the baby or him, honesty or humour? After that, I would draw an imaginary line down the middle of our bed. He wasn't allowed to cross it because if he did, I wouldn't get any sleep. When we woke, he would erase the imaginary line, pulling me close to him with one sweep of his arm. He smelt nice. Sometimes I could barely breathe.

Each week, the therapist began by asking us if we'd heard any difficult sounds and how we had dealt with them.

'Beautiful,' she'd say sympathetically after every story.

When we talked about holidays, I told them about the week I'd spent in Barcelona with the guy who bit his nails. After four days of pent-up frustration, a mugger hit me on the head while I was walking down the street at night, which made me pass out for a moment and left me with a wounded head.

'After that, I suddenly found myself able to relax,' I said.

'Oh,' said the therapist. She giggled. 'Great story, but where is it going?'

This almost made me cry. Probably also because I hadn't slept well in months. I was constantly having to get up at night to breastfeed Bob. When I put him on my breast, he'd fall asleep. When I put him down, he'd cry.

Bob's lip-smacking endeared him to me, but Arthur's noises made me nervous. The dust bunnies under the table and crumbs on the counter made me restless. Arthur often forgot to clean underneath the cutting board. There were germs on the garbage bin that could make us sick. Arthur complained that my hands were raw from all the scrubbing. I said that it was only the tips of my fingers and that the rest of me was still as soft as it had been when we met. At the time, he'd said that no one was softer than me. Now Bob was the softest. When we had nothing else to do, we'd each grab one of Bob's legs and gently squeeze it.

I'd asked Arthur to smack his lips into my phone's microphone so I could record it. The therapist told me I had to use computer programs to transform the sound into something that gave me peace, like a babbling brook, for example.

'Beautiful,' she said when I played it for the group. Kees had also chosen to use the sound of babbling water. He'd taken his telephone to a brook in the forest behind his house to record it.

'The only problem is that you can hear the sound of the highway,' he said. 'And I find that incredibly irritating.'

The therapist explained our new homework to us: we had to make a film linking difficult sounds to positive imagery. She played us an example, a film showing the same girl hanging in a parachute, linking arms with Mickey Mouse at Disneyland, and wearing a bikini on the beach. Accompanying the film was the rhythmic crunching of someone eating potato chips.

Arthur had a cold. I held my breath. Some of his coughs sounded angry, some sounded defeated, desperate or disappointed. He said I was reading too much into it.

'You've become one of those women who is always

bitching,' he also said. I was taking a cherry-pit heating pad out of the microwave for Bob, who was lying in my arms, sleeping. I threw the heating pad at Arthur's face, he slapped me, Bob cried.

'What's wrong with you?' Arthur screamed. I'd only seen him like this once before, when I was hugely pregnant and a man in the bus had refused to give up his seat for me. 'You can't handle motherhood,' he was now saying. I shouted back that he should shut his mouth, then grabbed his face and forcefully pressed his lips together. He pushed my hand away and went outside. Half an hour later, he was back.

'Sorry,' he said.

'Sorry,' I said too.

He kissed my face and my neck, then accidentally kissed my ear.

'If you ever completely lost it,' I asked Arthur, 'what would you lean into?'

'What do you mean?'

'You'd probably spend all your time looking at funny pictures,' I said. 'Or picking fights on the internet.'

'Yeah.' He was on his knees, bending over the modem. It had been glitching for a while, and if the internet was too slow, he wouldn't be able to follow his course on argumentation theory. An American university posted the lessons online for free. He used a dedicated online student discussion board to communicate with others about his weekly assignments. Sometimes it got out of hand. Arthur wasn't so good at dealing with people who couldn't think independently and parroted other people's scientific theories without questioning them. 'Always check which sources a person uses to inform their narrative,' he said. He also didn't love the moral judgement that underpinned most widely accepted beliefs. The idea that Jewish people were only ever good and all Nazis were pure evil was something that had bothered him even as a child. In those days, as a thought experiment, and to challenge black-and-white thinkers, he often deliberately defended unpopular opinions at school. But people who tried to extoll the virtues of the natural world annoyed him most of all. 'AIDS is also a natural phenomenon,' he would say.

When we first met, we'd sometimes argue about my acupuncturist, who relieved my stress once a month. 'It's never been proven that kind of treatment actually works,' Arthur would usually begin. Then I would say that I knew of people whose symptoms had completely disappeared, thanks to acupuncture. 'That's anecdotal evidence,' he'd say. To which I would reply that not everything had to be based on facts and that sometimes, you could just trust your own experience. 'Feelings can betray you!' he'd shout in response.

We were told to eat the snacks our therapist had put on the table while we discussed our homework, which had been a writing assignment. Kees had found it confronting to write about his childhood. His father had regularly punished him by making him stand in the corner and face the wall during dinner. He said his parents and brothers chewed and swallowed their food as if their lives depended on it. After his youngest brother died, they had spoken very little at the table. His brother had been hit by a truck while on his way to school with Kees. Marleen said she had written about the sexual abuse she'd endured as a child, but she didn't want to talk about it.

I picked up a carrot and took a bite. 'I think I made a mistake,' I said. My voice shook and my heart started thumping. Quickly, I swallowed the carrot. 'I didn't find the assignment confronting at all.' I'd described all of my father's eating techniques and the way my mother would watch him while he ate and then speak with an angry tone. She said she didn't speak with an angry tone, but she almost always did. Over time, the focus of our conversations shifted to my angry tone and my mother's tone grew less apparent.

The therapist nodded and asked Jona what she had written.

'Nothing,' said Jona. 'I didn't have enough time.' The previous weekend, she'd taken some kind of spiritual drug that made her vomit but had also given her a great deal of insight.

'Beautiful,' said the therapist. 'Do you want to expand upon that?'

Brian had attended a family dinner that he wasn't looking

forward to but had managed to withstand surprisingly well, though that was probably because he had deliberately chosen not to sit next to his sister, who made the same crackling sounds as his girlfriend when she ate.

I said I was getting better at tolerating difficult noises during dinner, but Arthur sometimes made lip-smacking sounds when he wasn't eating. They always sounded the same. I tried to copy him so I could figure out exactly what he was doing, but it was hard to assess whether these sounds were necessary or not.

The therapist ended the session by listing all the techniques we had learned. We used our phones to take pictures of the list so we would never forget them.

I swore as I struggled to get the seat belt around the Maxi-Cosi. Bob and I were going to stay at my father's place for the night. The last time I'd seen him was the day after Bob was born. He had stood beside the incubator crying and stroking Bob's cheek with his index finger until visiting hours were over. When I asked him why Margaret hadn't come with him, he told me that he was seeing a little less of her. 'Bob has your mother's mouth. It's exactly the same,' he kept repeating.

'Don't die,' said Arthur before I left. On the way, Bob started crying, and I stopped at a service station to feed him. Thankfully, he drank well. Every so often he would detach from my breast and look at me very seriously. While we were looking at each other, someone nearby slammed their car door. I watched fear enter Bob's eyes then slowly ebb away. He doesn't hide anything yet, I thought, smoothing the frown from his forehead with my finger.

When I drove into my father's street, he came outside and gestured wildly, guiding me into the driveway. Once we were inside, he was proud to show me the baby corner he'd set up in my old bedroom, complete with a cot, a chest filled with Lego, and a whole collection of stuffed animals. In the living room, there was a projector on a stand and a screen above the fireplace. He'd planned an evening of watching old family films together 'now that you're a mother'.

'Let me put on my glasses,' my father said when I put Bob on his lap. He spoke to the baby in the imaginary language that he'd originally made up for our dog. The dog was always stretched out across my father's chest in the evenings while he sat in his recliner in front of the television. It wasn't a small dog. According to my mother, my father would sometimes lie like that with me, until I grew too old for it.

'Until you started getting snappy,' she used to say, while she knew very well that the snapping started much later.

'Let's go to beddiebeddiebeddie,' said my father while putting Bob to bed.

During dinner I focused on the sounds from the street, the ticking of the clock and my own breath, a technique I learned at the madhouse.

My father told me about Margaret. 'She let me do my

own thing far too much,' he said. 'Which made me miss your mother even more.' My mother's things were still all over the house. Boxes filled with her collection of old glasses were blocking the pantry door. I was sure that my father had no idea what was in them, because he hit the boxes with the door all the time. There was no trace of Margaret.

After dinner, we watched my mother on the beach. She waved and held up the book she was reading: *Against Interpretation* by Susan Sontag. I thought about the weeks before her death, when she could no longer make it to the toilet, and my father had to wipe her bottom. I didn't know if I'd be able to do that if Arthur got to that stage, but when he'd had an ulcer the year before, I had ridden my bike all over the city to buy special sweets for him, the only sweets that didn't hurt his stomach. Arthur would probably be able to change my nappy without gagging. He could swallow any bad feelings that came up. Sometimes I heard him doing it. If I brought up a difficult subject, he'd go quiet, take a deep breath, swallow, then change the subject.

A little later we saw my mother and me in the forest with the dog. My mother was posing, and I was standing behind a tree. Come now, she gestured. In another film, I stared grumpily at the camera while my mother crouched down beside me. We were sitting in the garage, she said something and I shook my head resolutely. She opened the garage door, and I shook my head again. 'Do it for me,' is probably what she said.

When my mother used to send me out to play with the

girls who lived in the house behind ours, I'd often sneak into our garage and stay there trying to do a puzzle that was technically too complicated for me, but if I was patient and started with the corners it would eventually work itself out. When it came to the girls next door, I was less certain of my approach. Sometimes they were nice to me, but there were other days, when they whispered to each other or hid from me for an entire afternoon when we played hide and seek.

'You don't have a suit of armour,' said my mother. 'You need to get yourself some armour.'

For as long as she lived, she believed there was still hope for me, which is why she'd put in so much extra effort in her last few years. When I started high school, she encouraged me to take drama lessons, but I didn't know what to do with my arms when I was performing.

'Just let them dangle,' said my mother. 'Relax for once.'

In an effort to reassure her, I told her about a moment I remember vividly. I was around six years old and standing in front of the house next to the lavender bush, wearing my favourite dress. 'The light blue one with the flowers on it,' I said. The sun was shining, and I inhaled the scent of lavender. I'm happy now, I thought, I need to remember this moment.

'Exactly,' said my mother. 'That's what happens when you relax.'

In the final film my father played for us, I'd just been born, and we watched my mother lying in bed with me. I thought she looked even more beautiful without make-up.

'She was only twenty-five here,' said my father, 'thirteen

years younger than you are now.' I realised then that I was almost as old as my mother when she died.

For several minutes we watched shaky footage from different angles, showing my mother and me gazing deeply into each other's eyes. After that, my father turned off the projector.

The next morning, I told my father about the madhouse. He asked if Arthur's lip-smacking was the only thing that bothered me.

'Other people's lip-smacking bothers me as well,' I said.

He told me about a former patient of his, a woman who got anxious whenever she heard pigeons cooing. This was because her father had put birdseed in her pram whenever they went for a walk.

'Her father thought that was funny,' he said.

I said it was so easy to traumatise your child that occasionally I was almost tempted to do it. Together, we looked at Bob.

After lunch, I called Arthur to say that we were on our way.

'I love you,' he said, and when I asked him why, he said he didn't need a reason. He also told me he'd eaten four bagels with cream cheese, then stuck his fingers down his throat.

'There's no need to worry,' he said. 'I used to do it quite a lot when I lived alone.'

When I lived alone, I used to shuffle down to the supermarket every single day only to stand despairingly in front of the pre-cut vegetables. At night, I'd ask myself what it was that made people not want to stay in a relationship with me, if I should speak louder and be more expressive. But whenever I tried to do that, my eyes would fill with tears, even if I was happy about something. Then I'd have to look down and wait until my tears dried.

I rarely found myself alone anymore, but if I did, I'd wipe down the counter and garbage bin with a wet cloth, then lie on the couch and wait for the sadness to come. It no longer lived at the top of my throat, but had settled somewhere in my chest.

'If you ever completely lost it, you'd probably get quite angry,' Arthur once said to me. I found it more likely that I'd cry about everything. I'd cry about Arthur's collection of miniature Mexican skeletons, and the way he would say 'we are one' to me, then sheepishly laugh, and the five bottles of whiskey he'd bought because they were discounted, then immediately dropped two while carrying them home on his bike, and the way he sang along to David Bowie when he thought no one could hear him. I'd cry because, unlike a lot of people, he didn't look like a rodent, because he stuck his head out of the window whenever he heard a scooter alarm, and because of his pride when he saw Bob yawn for the first time. And about my father, who always made me a sweet omelette when I visited him, who used his cotton handkerchief to clean everything, who watched a Dutch soap opera every evening at eight o'clock, and had put a photo of Bob next to the photo of my mother on his desk. About the way Bob fully succumbed to sleep in my arms, his serious eyes, the way he chuckled when I counted out loud for him, when I'd counted to one hundred at least a hundred times. And I would cry for my mother.

'But you already cry a lot,' said Arthur. 'Bob gets it from you.'

While I put Bob in the Maxi-Cosi, my father asked if I was managing to keep it together.

'What a strange question,' I said.

'Yes,' he said, sounding tired, 'I'm a strange old man.'

I started tugging on the seatbelts.

'Goodbye, potato,' he said to Bob, 'Little potato from the potato farm. Please take good care of your Mama.'

Don't Lie

I stood on the balcony looking out at the courtyard. Children were squealing, there was a barbeque happening nearby, someone on the other side of the courtyard was laughing nervously, and directly beneath me a woman was talking in a loud voice about something that wasn't her problem.

When I was nine, I wished I could win a prize that consisted of me being able to look inside everyone's house. It would mean that I could just ring any random doorbell I wanted. Whoever opened the door would step back and say: 'Oh, it's the prize-winner, please go ahead and look around.' I'd look for their family photos, which can usually be found hanging on the walls in the hallway or somewhere in the living room, like the sideboard or windowsills. I would cover all the smiling mouths with my hand and look closely at their eyes.

A few years later, I went through a phase of wanting to be a police detective. People would come to see me in my office, hoping I could help them understand their lover's suspicious behaviour. First, I'd assess how likely it was that their allegations were true. Had there been any unusual behaviour? I'd look for clues in recent photos of their lovers. The rest of the evidence would be gleaned from their responses to my questions: How often did the suspect laugh? What kind of birthday presents did he give you? How did he respond if he accidentally dropped something? Did he often say that dinner was a disaster? And I would wear a long raincoat and red boots.

'You mean a private detective,' said my father. According to him, you should never let other people know that you had them figured out. 'Sometimes they don't even know that they're maintaining a façade,' he said. His questions usually began with the words: Is it possible ... 'If it turns out that it isn't, then you can always take it back.' This worked well with his patients. Sometimes, he'd say to my mother: 'I notice that you're getting agitated. Is it possible that you're angry about something?'

'No,' my mother would shout in response. 'It isn't possible!'

The day before what would have been her sixty-fifth birthday, my father called and asked if Arthur, Bob and I would like to come and stay overnight with him. 'Arthur has to work,' I said. 'But I'll come with Bob and organise the birthday cake.'

Ever since my mother's death, my father had bought a blueberry cheesecake on her birthday, but it never tasted the same as the ones she used to make. He'd tried all the bakeries in the area, but this year I had made a cake.

It was in a box in the back of the car, wedged between a suitcase and the folded pram, so it wouldn't slide around. I parked carefully in front of my father's house and carried the cake inside. In the meantime, my father freed Bob from his car seat. The art deco cake stand was already sitting on the table. I was able to slide the cake onto the stand without damaging it. Then I took off my coat and sat down. My father took a seat on the other side of the table and waited patiently until Bob was installed in the chair next to him before cutting the cake into slices. He took a big bite, and then another one.

'It's a little too sweet,' he said with his mouth full.

I took a bite.

'You're right,' I said. 'It's a disaster.'

Bob stuck his finger in the blueberry jam and licked it. Then he leaned over his plate and sank his teeth into the cake.

'Look at him go,' said my father.

After the cake, I asked my father if I could have the cufflinks he had worn at his wedding, because I wanted to give them to Arthur. He said that he couldn't remember owning any cufflinks, but if they existed, I could have them. And he said that he'd had to open almost every box in the garage, but he'd finally found his old camera. For my wedding, he said. Now he could film everything.

'But I don't want you to,' I said. 'I've told you that at least fifty times.'

The cufflinks were lying in the drawer where he kept his ties. He never opened that drawer. I also found the miniature bronze copy of Rodin's *The Kiss* that my parents had bought in Paris during their honeymoon. It was badly glued together.

For years, the miniature statue had stood on a cabinet in our hallway. Whenever I looked at it, I was struck by the feeling that there was something I wasn't part of, something I didn't quite understand. It reminded me of the night I turned four, when I couldn't get to sleep because of all the excitement. On my way to the toilet, I heard the TV in the living room and went to have a look. There, on the rug in front of the couch, I saw a heaving lump of flesh. My father's head suddenly popped out of the lump. He'd never looked at me with such disapproval. Then the lump fell apart, and I saw my mother. She was lying underneath my father with her legs in the air. The sound of applause emanated from the TV.

But I loved that little statue. It held a secret. I often reached out to touch it when I was passing by, but one day I wasn't paying attention and accidentally knocked it off the cabinet with my bag. There was a heavy thud followed by a deep silence. The statue had broken in half and was lying at my feet. My father was standing in the hall, and we looked at each other in bewilderment.

Before I understood how important it was to look people in the eye, I thought you could tell from their forehead whether they were telling the truth or not, and that was the reason my mother had a thick fringe. 'A little dot appears on your forehead whenever you tell a lie,' she always said. At night, she'd sit on the edge of my bed, and I'd ask her questions.

'Why does Papa's breath smell so bad?'
'Because he drinks too much.'
'Would you rather get run over or be cut into pieces?'
'Run over.'
'What happens when your nose runs out of snot?'
'Then you'll never catch another cold.'

I picked my nose constantly for a while but stopped when it became apparent that I was still catching colds. This was also around the time that my mother had an affair.

His name was Clark, just like Superman when he was undercover. He was from Suriname and eight years younger than my mother. She smiled when she told me about him a few weeks before she died.

'I remember exactly how we met,' she said. He had been sitting opposite her on the train. 'Your eyes,' he kept repeating. He had to see her again. They saw each other fifteen times in five months, while I was at school and my father was at the institution. Their final meeting was on a Sunday, while my father, the dog and I were taking our weekly walk through the forest. She'd driven him to the station at five o'clock, and they'd sat for a few minutes in the car. At that same moment, my father and I would have been sitting near the food truck at the edge of the forest, about to eat two sausages and a serving of loaded fries.

Clark had slammed his fist on the dashboard. 'Don't do this,' he said to my mother. 'Come home with me.' My mother had fiddled with the button on her jacket until it had come loose and rolled under the car seat. After Clark had left, she'd spent a long time searching for it.

Arthur and I got married on a Thursday. My father tripped on the doorstep at the town hall and dropped his camera.

'I can film it,' said Arthur's father. 'I have an iPhone.'

After the ceremony, we dined with our families at the hotel where Arthur's father had worked until his retirement. He'd arranged a room for Arthur and me as a surprise wedding present.

'It's a premium extra-large room with a view,' he said, as if he were still the manager. He handed us the key. My father would stay at our house with Bob.

'You guys don't have to do a thing,' he said. 'I brought my own duvet.'

Arthur's father stood up during the first course and held a little piece of paper close to his face.

'Ladies and Gentlemen,' he read. Arthur's sister sighed. First, we were given a summary of Arthur's career, how he didn't finish school and had gone on to live a fairly horizontal existence, lying around at home on the couch or, if someone wanted to sit on the couch, on the ground. And we were told that he hadn't followed in his father's footsteps, but, eventually, it had all worked out, more or less.

'But today, we aren't here to talk about work,' he concluded, 'we're here to celebrate love.' He raised his bushy eyebrows and looked at us. 'Arthur, you're so lucky to have such a lovely wife. Cheers to your lovely wife,' he said, raising his glass in the air.

After this, my father stood. He coughed.

'It's a shame your mother couldn't be here today,' he said. For a moment, he fell silent and stared at the house-made croquette on his plate before sitting down again. 'I'll continue a bit later,' he said. 'The food is getting cold.' Bob had already eaten almost all of his croquette.

After the first course, my father stood again and started telling an elaborate story about the day that he heard I was pregnant. He'd just poured himself a glass of whiskey when I called him with the news. 'This is the most beautiful gift you could give us,' he'd said, then corrected himself. 'I mean me. That you could give me.' After this, he drank his entire glass of whiskey and immediately poured himself another. 'I was drunk as a skunk by the end of the phone call,' he said. 'And incredibly happy and sad.'

He looked up for a moment.

'More,' said Bob. 'More croquettes!'

'Your mother would have really loved becoming a grandmother,' said my father, 'even though she didn't like the word itself. The first time I ever laid eyes on her was back when I was still working behind the bar at that student café.' My father told this story whenever he got the chance. That he'd been wiping down the bar when he suddenly looked up and saw her standing in front of him. With those eyes of hers. Not blue, but turquoise. And that he'd kept polishing that bar with his cloth, so she'd had to call out twice to get his attention and order from him. The way she pronounced the 'i' in 'wine' was so refined and rarely heard, and she kept looking around the room as if lost. He wanted nothing more than to stroke her fashionable hair and tell her that it was all going to be okay. 'It took some time for her to give me a chance,' said my father, 'and it's been almost thirty years since she died, but in some sense, since that night, she has always been with me.' And he wished the same for us, but without one of us having to die while we were still young. 'You guys aren't that young anymore,' he said, 'so you've got that going for you.'

We drank to that. During the main course, Arthur's mother said that she'd never had such a lovely evening at the hotel. And we also drank to that, and we drank to the rain outside and the candlelight inside and the red, kimono-style dress that Arthur's mother was wearing, which only just avoided catching fire. After dessert, while drinking cognac, my father and Arthur's mother started singing a protest song from the sixties that was supposed to be sung fast and staccato, and concluded with a long wail that only ended when Bob knocked over my father's glass.

'Oh, damn it,' said Arthur's mother.

'He needs to go to bed,' I said.

'One more song,' said my father.

There was champagne in a bucket of ice on our bedside table.

'I can't go on,' said Arthur, throwing himself on the extra-large bed. I went into the bathroom to take out my contact lenses and when I returned, he was still lying there, face down in a heart made of red rose petals. There were also petals on the floor surrounding the bed.

'Wake up,' I said. 'We're married.'

The telephone rang softly. The receptionist asked if my husband had left his watch in the restaurant.

'No,' I said. 'My husband doesn't wear a watch. My husband never wants to know what time it is.' It was eleven-thirty. This is my husband, I thought. He's sleeping. I opened the bottle of champagne, which woke Arthur.

'Do you want some?' I asked.

'No.' He turned over. 'Actually, maybe I do.'

'Are you annoyed?'

He shook his head.

'Don't lie,' I said.

He laughed. 'Why do you always say that?'

I put our glasses on the bedside table and let myself fall onto the bed next to Arthur. Together, we rocked back and forth.

'It's a waterbed,' I said.

'My father was the one who ordered all these beds,' said Arthur, 'when he was still working here.' He swears by waterbeds.

'Oh, yeah, of course. Your parents have one too.'

'My father says they're relaxing.'

The bed woke me up at five am. It was shuddering because someone had come to lie next to me.

'Arthur?' I whispered. I'd recently seen a movie about a demon baby that lived in the cellar and crept into people's beds at night.

'Yes.' It was Arthur.

'How do you think it's going with Bob?' I asked. 'My father was really drunk.'

'I think it's going well,' said Arthur. He crept towards me and pulled me closer.

A little later, when I was trying to get back to sleep, I kept hearing the same song in my head. It had been in my head for ten years. At first, I would hear it every day, but in the past few years I'd only thought of it every so often, when my father talked about his time doing military service in the south of France and once when I was crying over the washing up after a fight with Arthur. It was the refrain from a song by Simon & Garfunkel. Lailailai, it went, lailailailailailai. Lailailai. Lailailailailailailailalalalalai. Arthur and I had made up as soon as I finished the washing up. Now he was snoring, and I was sprinkling rose petals all over his body.

Back at home, Bob was sitting on the floor, piling up books in front of the bookshelf. My father was lying on the couch with his eyes shut.

'Are you asleep?' I asked.

'No,' he said, struggling to sit up. 'I didn't sleep a wink all night.' He sounded just like my mother, who never slept. She complained about it, but never wanted to see a doctor. 'Then I don't want to hear another thing about it,' I'd often tell her.

Bob hadn't kept him awake, my father said. It was his own mind, he'd been lying there worrying about things. 'That happens every now and then,' he said. 'Recently, it's been happening quite a lot.'

'You should meditate,' I said. 'You know that, right?' I'd been saying this regularly to my father since I'd completed a ten-day silent meditation retreat. At the meditation centre, I shared a room with another woman. Every night I dreamt about someone I'd been angry with. On our last night, I had trouble falling asleep because my roommate's bed kept creaking. I suspected she was masturbating.

This was long before I met Arthur and Bob even existed.

'He hit me in the face when I got him out of bed this

morning,' said my father, 'but apart from that he was very sweet.'

Bob looked up from his books and nodded.

'And that's a wrap on the best day of your life,' said my father when we were saying goodbye.

One of the best days of my life was the day that I stood in the schoolyard wearing a long, light blue puffer jacket my mother had bought for me. The older brother of the boy I was secretly in love with had ridden past on his bike.

'The tall one over there wearing the duvet,' he'd called out to his friend. 'That's the one my brother really likes.'

A few months later, I was at school camp with the rest of my class, and we were staying in a wood cabin in the forest. Next to the cabin was a shed where the boy who really liked me spent hours with my best friend. The two of them would crouch behind a pile of boxes whenever I went into the shed.

'I'm just not likeable enough,' I said to my mother once I was home again. She was busy brushing all the knots out of my hair, pressing the brush roughly into my scalp.

'You are likeable,' she said. 'Don't say that ever again.'

When my mother spoke about her wedding day, she'd get tears in her eyes. She should never have dropped out of acting school. The fact that she was pregnant and marrying a non-believer was a huge disappointment for her parents. But they went to her wedding anyway.

'A good parent always puts their child first,' said my

father a few years later when her parents chose Jehovah after all and withdrew from our lives. A good wife puts her husband first, I thought when my mother told me about Clark. According to my father, she'd completely made up the story about Clark. He'd come to my bedroom just to tell me this. I was studying French vocabulary, my finger resting on the words 'tremblement de terre', when he walked in. He stood in the middle of the room, leaning on one leg with his hand in his pocket. Hallucinations are very common when you are dying, he said. And fantasies are a bit like that.

'And you know, your mother always had a good imagination, right?'

At her acting school, they said she looked like Romy Schneider. At home, when she smoked her Gauloises, she'd gaze enigmatically into space as if being filmed for a close-up. The camera followed her everywhere, in the same way that Jehovah was always watching her parents and Sinterklaas was watching me. We were sitting in a schnitzel restaurant when my parents told me that Sinterklaas didn't exist.

'I knew it,' I said. My heart was thumping. That white beard wasn't real, it was a costume. How had I never noticed. Even my father had once donned that costume, to celebrate Sinterklaas at his institution one afternoon. I'd sat quietly on his lap and politely answered all his questions.

'You were scared of him,' said my mother. 'It was so sweet.'

○

'I used to be the Dutch junior tapdancing champion,' said Arthur, 'in the ten to fourteen category.' We looked at Bob, who was dancing on the rug in front of the TV.

'Really?' I asked.

'No, of course not. You actually will believe anything.'

'I'm a lovely wife,' I said. 'That's what your father said.'

'When did he say that?'

'In his speech, yesterday.'

'Oh, yes, that,' said Arthur.

'To your lovely wife,' I said, holding my glass of wine in the air.

'To my wife,' he said. 'Who is the loveliest.' He went over and stood next to Bob then rhythmically tapped the heels and toes of his sneakers on the floor.

Bye

We put her in the living room, so she could see the garden. It had been snowing that day.

'Put on your scarf,' she said when I went outside. She was lying under a thick blanket wearing a beanie.

There were quite a few footprints in the snow. I followed the prints with the most familiar profile. Most fathers wore rubber boots or put waterproof covers over their shoes, but my father had classic brown leather boots that my mother had bought him in a little Italian mountain village we'd once visited on holiday. A few days earlier, they had managed to resolve a massive argument, and we'd all felt a little dizzy from the altitude and our relief.

At the end of the driveway, the trail of my father's feet had been trampled over by other footprints. A car drove slowly along the street and stopped beside me. The neighbour wound down his car window.

'Don't you go to school anymore?' he asked.

'Yes, I'm still going today, but I had the first hour off.'

'Is your father home?'

'No, he went to the supermarket, but the nurse is there.'

He said that he and his wife would come once he finished work, at around five-thirty, to say their goodbyes. He worked at the town council and would come home for lunch every day. According to my mother, this was because his wife didn't like to be alone. She was quite anxious. And the reason she was so thin was because she always had diarrhoea.

At school, I found my friend by the back door, talking to an older girl who lived in a group home. Both sides of her head were shaved, and she was wearing dark eyeshadow and a Palestinian scarf. My mother said I should call it a keffiyeh — she sympathised with the Palestinian Liberation movement and believed it was wrong to wear them casually. But I wanted one anyway. I'd seen a really beautiful purple keffiyeh, which I was planning on buying once my mother died. My friend asked me where I had been. There was a tiny droplet clinging to her nose.

The neighbours arrived at five-thirty. The woman was holding a bunch of tulips, which she used to cover her crotch when the dog went over to greet her.

'Yesss,' she said. 'Smell these instead.' She told my mother that the garden looked so bare and bleak in the winter. Then she quickly started talking about our lavender bush and how she would prune it for us in the spring. My father excused himself. He had to go and pick up some soup at a friend's house. It was the only thing my mother would still eat. Starting tomorrow, she had decided to stop eating. When the neighbour finished talking about the garden, she turned to look at me. 'If you ever need anything,' she said, 'you can always knock on our door.' Her husband nodded gravely, and my mother said: 'If she ever wants to eat something other than an omelette.'

I plucked a piece of lint off my sweater. Maybe my mother had forgotten what she always said about the neighbour's microwave meals. When my father returned, they finally stood up to go.

'Yes,' said the neighbour.

'Bye,' said my mother.

'Bye,' said the neighbour's husband.

Then both of them shook her hand.

I slept through the alarm.

'Why didn't you wake me?' I asked my father.

'Why would I?'

My mother's eyes were closed. I didn't know if it was appropriate to eat around her. My father was sitting in his recliner with his crossword book in his left hand, using his right hand to spoon porridge out of the bowl on his lap.

'Should I take your plate for you?' I asked when I stood up to go to the kitchen.

'You don't have to whisper, you know,' he said brightly.

I looked at my mother again. She hadn't moved at all.

The nurse came in through the back door. My mother had told me she was a lesbian and had a girlfriend who lived with her. I'd seen the girlfriend once, when she'd driven down our street. So they probably scissor, I thought.

The nurse was called Sis. She had a tiny plant mister that she used to wet my mother's lips. My father grabbed the mister and was about to take it over to my mother, but Sis stopped him.

'Don't do it too often,' she said. She called the plant mister a nebuliser, and asked if we could buy our own because she had to take hers home with her at the end of the day.

'Okiedokie,' said my father.

There was still snow on the ground, so I decided to walk to the shops instead of taking my bike. I passed my old primary school along the way. It had only been a year since I'd been in that schoolyard. I saw a teacher standing beside the monkey bars talking to a group of boys with his hands on his hips. It was the same teacher I'd once complained to about a boy who had taken my marbles.

'Which boy?' he had asked.

'The Turk,' I said, but the teacher told me I should have said the Turkish boy. My father reassured me later that you could just say Turk when referring to Turks.

'It is a nationality,' he said.

'A fine nationality,' my mother emphasised. She was

determined never to judge anyone on their background, only their behaviour. This boy — who was probably both Dutch and Turkish she wanted to add, was I listening? — had taken my marbles, but eventually he'd also given them back.

The school was situated on a wide main road. Half of my classmates lived in the flats on the same side of the road as the school and the other half lived on our side, in the bungalows owned by doctors, academics and civil servants. Behind these houses was where the forest began.

The pharmacy stocked plant misters in several different sizes.

'Is it for smaller or larger plants?' asked the shop assistant.

'It's for my mother,' I said.

The woman blinked and smiled politely. My mother and I always used to imitate her.

'Shall we go for the large one then?' she said. She picked up a brown plant mister that was the same size as my lower arm.

'Let's do this one,' I said, picking up the smallest one.

'Byeee,' said the sales assistant once I had paid.

'Byeee,' I said.

I asked my mother if she was hungry.

'No, darling,' she said in a soft voice. Maybe she found some satisfaction in no longer consuming any calories. She'd always counted them, but she'd never eaten less than one thousand calories a day, unless she had the flu or was doing one of her juice cleanses. It annoyed her that she hadn't lost any weight from chemotherapy.

'Shall I read to you?' I asked and picked up the book she'd recently started reading. She had read up to chapter twelve. The main protagonist had drunk all the wine in his house and was looking for more. Against his better judgement, he searched all his secret hiding places and was standing next to the kitchen cupboard when he was suddenly overcome by a wavy of self-pity. His mother was dead, and no one loved him. Except his boyfriend, which was somewhat comforting. But it was entirely possible that his boyfriend had a secret lover he met when he said he was going to his classes at university. He'd like to see the guy. Even a crumpled passport photo would be enough. 'The idea of this other person filled Treger with a voracious, almost painfully greedy sense of pleasure,' I read. Treger was his name. His boyfriend was called Unicorn. My mother liked names like that. Treger then imagined that his boyfriend's lover could grow tired of him. '*He's going to hurt Unicorn, just for the fun of it*, thought Treger. *That dirty, little ass-whore.*' I glanced at my mother, but she still hadn't drifted off. In the kitchen cupboard, behind the salad dressing, Treger discovered a bottle of red wine that Unicorn must have bought and hidden. He wondered if his boyfriend would notice that the bottle was missing. '*Ach, I can have a little something for myself too*, Treger thought. *What do I have? Nothing, absolutely nothing and that's the truth of it.*'

Once my mother was asleep, I crept into the kitchen where Sis was leafing through a magazine.

'Go and do something fun,' she said. 'I'll look after things here.' My father was resting after another sleepless night. I went to my room and called my friend, who told me that the drama club at school was putting on a production of *Romeo and Juliet*, and she was going to play Juliet. She wanted to know if she could ask my mother for acting tips.

'It's essential that you breathe deeply and slowly,' I said. 'That's what she always told me to do. And you have to magnify yourself. Not just your body, your energy too.' My friend tried not to laugh. She wanted to know if my mother had ever played Juliet, but I didn't know. 'She did play the lead in a police procedural,' I said, 'but that was before I was born.'

When my mother woke up, I told her about *Romeo and Juliet* and my friend. She'd never played that role, she said, but she had starred in a police procedural.

'I played the lead role, you know,' she said.

My father was sitting at the end of my bed, crying. I rubbed his back and thought about the last time we'd sat on my bed like this. I was six, and I'd had a dream about a giant snake who slithered from the city centre, down the main road and into our driveway. My father had been sitting in the garden reading the paper when the snake swallowed him. I had woken up crying, and my father had come into my bedroom, sat on my bed and stroked my back, just as I was now stroking his back. His shirt felt clammy. He was trembling and trying to say something.

'It's okay,' I said, 'I understand.'

Once he calmed down, we went into the living room and pulled our old photo albums from the bookshelf.

'Look, Ma,' I said, 'this was when you wore that ridiculous bikini.' I held the photo up in front of her.

'Her eyesight is getting worse,' said my father. 'You should tell her what is in the photo.'

'Let me see it,' said my mother. She sounded almost angry, like she used to. I held up the photo again, this time a little closer to her face. 'Oh, yes,' she whispered and closed her eyes.

I was happy she wasn't speaking as much. A few weeks ago, she'd suddenly started telling me about a secret love affair she'd had. Then, just as abruptly, she'd stopped talking about it. My father also had no explanation for why she was behaving normally again. He'd looked through his old medical textbooks but hadn't been able to find any information on it.

Sis arrived, my father went to sleep, and I took the dog outside for a walk. I was wearing my sneakers, and we ran across the poop field behind all the houses to the forest where I stood panting for a moment. Then I looked around to see if I was alone before screaming as hard as I could. Something shrill came out of my throat. The dog was sniffing a tree nearby. Feel your feet, I thought, bend your knees slightly and breathe all the way down to your anus. I screamed again and this time it sounded good.

At home, Freddy and Lea were sitting on my mother's bed. Freddy had been working as a psychotherapist at my father's institution for ten years. He had a bushy moustache. Lea wore long, loose hippie dresses that my mother said she was too old to wear. They used to visit us when we went to France in the summer, at the nudist campsite on the river. They were Jewish and had a daughter who was a little younger than me. The first summer they came to visit us, I made sure I was always walking behind her whenever we climbed over the boulders by the river. I wanted to look between her legs and see what it looked like when you were circumcised.

Freddy and Lea had brought us a large bundle of decorative autumn branches. They were arranged on the windowsill next to the neighbour's tulips, which were starting to droop. Lea was holding my mother's hand, and Freddy was talking about their daughter. She had just been told she qualified for VWO, the second-highest level of high school education. Both Freddy and Lea bent forward so they could hear what my mother was saying, which was that I had qualified for the highest level of high school, but I hadn't wanted to go because my friends were all going to do VWO, and it was a shame, especially because most of my friends hadn't been put in the same class as me. Lea said that was indeed a terrible shame, and Freddy added that their daughter was also smart enough to do the highest level of high school.

'She'll probably end up choosing to do it,' he said. The last time I'd seen their daughter, she had vomited all over my shoes after drinking her parent's wine with me at one of their parties.

After Freddy and Lea said goodbye, my mother's skin turned grey, except her nose, which looked like a pink beak sticking out of her hollow face. I asked her if she was cold.

'Do you remember when you always used to ask me that?' she said. 'You wanted me to say "Yes, I'm very cold" so that you could cuddle me and warm me up.'

'Shall I warm you up?'

'Yes,' she said. 'Fetch me another blanket.'

My father and I had just finished decorating the Christmas tree when the doorbell rang.

'Here we are again,' said an older man when I opened the door. He was in a suit. The old woman next to him was wearing a hat. 'You've grown so much,' he said. 'You were only this tall the last time I saw you.' He held his hand barely a metre off the ground.

'The last time we saw her was at Ibby's funeral,' the woman quickly added. 'That was four years ago.' That's when I realised who they were. My father came into the hallway.

'Oh,' he said. 'Has there been a new light?'

My grandmother looked at the ground, and my grandfather cleared his throat.

'We've come to pay our last respects,' he said. 'That's allowed.' His voice was now solemn.

My mother had once explained it all to me. Jehovah's Witnesses regularly received 'flashes of light' that contained 'the truth' and came directly from Jehovah himself, and they could mean that you were suddenly no longer allowed to celebrate Queen's Day or contact someone who'd been excommunicated from the church. And then, a few years later, you'd be allowed some contact with them, and a while after that, it would be forbidden again. But Jehovah's Witnesses also had a moral obligation to support their loved ones when they were grieving, even those they'd excommunicated. That had never changed.

My father let them in.

'Wait here a minute,' he said. 'I'll ask if it's okay.' My grandmother took off her hat and finessed her white hair. There was a mirror hanging in the hallway, but she kept her eyes fixed in front of her. My grandfather asked me how school was. He continued smiling and fiddled with his tie. He used to weave baskets with me, my mother had often said. I looked at the floor until my father returned. He held open the living room door.

My grandmother was shocked by the sight of my mother. As she took a seat beside the bed, she quickly wiped away her tears.

'My child,' said my grandfather in a soft voice. The last time they had sat in this room was when they came to tell us they could no longer see us. My mother still remembered exactly what had happened. They'd talked about the poor condition of the roads between their town and ours, and about the increasing numbers of Turks in the area, and they expressed their admiration for an ashtray I'd made out of clay. Then they said: 'There's a reason we've come here today.' And that was that.

My mother moved her dry lips in an effort to greet them. My father told them the latest news about my mother's illness.

'Probably just a few more days,' he said, 'before her heart gives up.'

'Yes,' said my grandfather. 'Yes, yes.'

It was quiet for a moment.

'It could still happen,' my grandmother spoke up. 'You could still enter paradise.'

My mother looked outside.

'I don't think you can expect her to repent anymore,' said my father.

Whenever my mother made a sound, my father would reach for the plant mister. He kept it on the floor next to his recliner. Sis felt it was time he got a proper night's sleep. I was going to watch over my mother.

She seemed to be feeling a little clearer. Maybe the visit from her parents earlier that day had woken her up.

'Your body produces adrenaline when you're angry,' said my father. Most of her friends had already said their goodbyes. My uncle was the only one who hadn't come to see her. He imported vintage cars from Florida and was supposed to return from Miami later that night.

I lay next to my mother in my father's recliner, which I had fully reclined. In the glow of Christmas lights, I looked at her face.

'Are you scared?' I asked.

She shook her head.

'Not now,' she said.

A few hours later I was woken by the dog, who had come in from the hallway because I'd forgotten to close the door. He sniffed at my feet and then lay down on the rug next to me. I heard my mother moaning softly.

'What's wrong?' I asked. She said that she wasn't lying comfortably. I used my right arm to hold her up while using my left to arrange the pillows beneath her head. 'Plop,' I said when I let her go and she fell with a thud back onto the pillows. She wanted to know what the first year of high school was like, what I did during breaks and which boys I liked. 'I don't like anyone,' I said, and told her that a lot of the girls bleached their hair and called me a snob because I didn't speak in the local dialect. Those girls called my sandals 'Turkish Nikes' and mostly hung out with my best friend, whose boyfriend was the most popular boy in the class. He'd once grabbed my boobs while walking past me, even though I barely had any boobs. No one criticised my friend for speaking standard Dutch. Sometimes she would go and do things with the blonde girls after school, and inevitably something would happen that would send them all into fits of giggles for days afterward. My mother asked if her asthma was still as bad and if her parents still left her alone all the time. My friend wanted to be a businesswoman, just like her mother, and she aspired to work for Shell at one of their offices in China. She also knew which university she wanted to attend.

'If only my child was that level-headed,' my mother would say to me every so often. To others she'd say: 'It's difficult for my daughter to choose because she's good at everything she does.'

'You're going to continue taking drama classes, aren't you?' she asked me now. 'You really must be part of the school production next year, unless your father happens to be dying or something.' When I didn't immediately answer, she said: 'Darling please, do it for me.'

My father sprayed a little water on my mother's mouth and looked at his watch. Sis still hadn't arrived, and it was ten o'clock. My mother needed to be washed.

'She'll come,' I said. 'Calm down.'

'I'll cut your nails in a minute,' he said to my mother. 'Before your brother gets here.' He looked at his watch again.

When Sis walked in, my mother was bent over my shoulder and my father was running a washcloth over her back.

'Don't rush it,' I said. My mother was breathing heavily.

I hoped she couldn't smell me. We'd had to move the flowers and the Christmas tree earlier that morning because she couldn't stand the scent of them anymore. When the doorbell rang, Sis took over from me.

My uncle's black Chevrolet was parked with its nose practically touching the back of our Toyota. It was a customised car that he could steer using just his left arm. He had lost his right arm on his way to school one day. The moveable bridge they usually crossed had been open to let a boat pass, and he'd been leaning on the mechanism that operated the lever, which had suddenly started to move. My mother had been standing right beside him, watching as his arm twisted. It had taken a long time for the lever to make its way back to the top.

'Hello, bug,' he said, shoving a plastic duty-free bag into my hands. 'For you.' Inside a box with a bow wrapped around it was a bottle of perfume. 'It's a unisex scent, so if you think your father stinks you can also spray it all over him.' I thought that sounded a bit gross. My uncle gave my father a plastic bag containing a bottle of whiskey. Then he went back to his car to get a big bunch of red roses and walked straight into the living room holding them. My mother was lying propped up in bed.

'How beautiful,' she said. My uncle stood timidly beside her bed holding the flowers. My father took them from him and put them in a bucket in the kitchen.

'She really cannot stand having those near her right now,' he said to me.

When I walked back into the room, my uncle was sitting with his head in his hands, sobbing. My mother was stroking his sleeve.

'Hey, it's okay,' she said. When my uncle was finished crying, my father told him about my grandparents' visit and the paradise that my mother was still eligible to enter.

'Imagine if paradise really exists,' said my mother.

'Maybe you should say sorry just in case,' said my uncle. He babbled about the past, how he'd playfully wrestle with his father, and afterwards, they'd both have imprints from the jute rug on their cheeks.

'He was a strange, sweet, funny, stubborn, vulnerable, smart, stupid man.'

'Is,' said my mother. 'He's still alive.'

'Was I a happy child?' He said that his therapist had advised him to ask that.

'You definitely were until you turned four,' said my mother. 'Up until you went to school. When you came home from school, you'd kick the front door until Mama opened it and then you'd kick her shins.'

He had to think about that for a moment.

She looked like a starving child: tiny, with thin limbs, a rounded belly, enormous eyes, and a wrinkled face. When I accidentally dropped her, she broke into lots of little pieces that slowly dissolved until only her head remained. She stared at me with those enormous eyes.

I got out of bed and walked into the living room.

'It's taking so long,' she whispered, as I pulled the duvet up to cover her shoulders. Her eyes remained closed.

There was a deer three bungalows down. It was standing in the garden of the architect who had just moved in, on the edge of his empty swimming pool, in the snow. She jumped when she saw me, then slipped and fell into the pool. I ran over to her. Panicking, she leapt and threw herself against the pool walls. I lay on the ground and held out my hand, but she didn't seem to understand. She kept slipping, and turning around and around. Suddenly, she leapt so high, and her head came so close to my face, that I could feel her breath. Then she slipped back down to the bottom and hurled herself even more wildly against the side of the pool, choosing the side that was furthest from me. It was the shallow end and there was a metal ladder. After leaping a few more times, she managed to fight her way out of the pool. Then she bounded away beautifully and disappeared through the hedge.

I ran home.

'Ma!' I cried. For a moment, I expected her to be sitting on the couch, talking on the phone. My father was sitting at her bedside. He looked up, disturbed, and put a finger to his lips.

'You know you're not supposed to shout,' he said. My

mother's eyes hadn't opened since the day before. I told my father about the deer.

'Don't you think that's a crazy story?' I whispered.

'Yes,' he said. 'I have to get something from the kitchen. Why don't you tell your mother.'

I was lying on the couch with the dog at my feet. My father was sitting in his chair beside the bed.

'I think it's time,' he said. I went and sat on the other side of the bed and stroked my mother's soft, short hair. Before she'd started her last round of chemo, I had shaved her head. We'd been listening to music, an American gospel choir. My mother sang along to the music while I did laps over her head with the clippers. Her voice had sounded thin and fragile alongside the deep voices of the gospel singers.

'Is she dead?' I asked.

My father held a mirror up to her mouth to see if it fogged. It did.

'Say something,' he said. 'Maybe she can still hear you.'

'Hi,' I said. Then I started laughing, which made me cry.

My great-aunt Ibby, who died after a long illness, spent her last few evenings thinking, *Tonight, I will go*, and every morning she'd wake up and say, 'Goddammit, I'm still here.' I didn't want to think about that. Suddenly, my mother sighed.

'Wait,' I said when my father reached for the nebuliser. We waited. My father crossed his legs, wiggled his foot, grabbed her hand, and stroked the bruising on her lower arm. I put my hand on her crown to keep her warm. And we stayed like that for some time.